Helen smiled

'Funny how it's ... ulcers. It's becaus... and won't talk to each other ... ... up and becomes intolerable.'

A fleeting shadow crossed Tom's face. 'Yes, very likely. Mind if I have a look at the post-ops?'

The sudden change of atmosphere was puzzling. Had he taken her remarks as criticism? She hoped he wasn't going to be all tetchy and theatrical — it would drive her mad.

Dear Reader

We're only travelling far with one book this month, as Lilian Darcy takes us cruising Bermudan waters in RUNNING AWAY. A MAN OF HONOUR by Caroline Anderson is a deeply moving book, while Jean Evans gives us her first vet book set on Jersey with THE FRAGILE HEART. Elizabeth Harrison gives us a hero with spinal injuries in THE SENIOR PARTNER'S DAUGHTER, all of which makes up a perfectly super month. Do enjoy!

The Editor

Caroline Anderson's nursing career was brought to an abrupt halt by a back injury, but her interest in medical things led her to work first as a medical secretary, and then, after completing her teacher training, as a lecturer in medical office practice to trainee medical secretaries. In addition to writing, she also runs her own business from her home in rural Suffolk, where she lives with husband, two daughters, mother and dog.

Recent titles by the same author:

PICKING UP THE PIECES
SECOND THOUGHTS

A MAN OF HONOUR

BY

CAROLINE ANDERSON

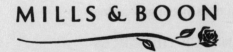

MILLS & BOON LIMITED
ETON HOUSE, 18–24 PARADISE ROAD
RICHMOND, SURREY, TW9 1SR

First published in Great Britain 1994
by Mills & Boon Limited

© Caroline Anderson 1994

Australian copyright 1994   Philippine copyright 1994
This edition 1994

ISBN 0 263 78590 4

Set in 10 on 12 pt Linotron Times
03-9405-52204

Typeset in Great Britain by Centracet, Cambridge
Made and printed in Great Britain

CHAPTER ONE

SHE didn't know what it was about him — in a department filled with attractive men, his regular features and easy, natural bearing were not particularly remarkable — but there was something compelling, some elusive, indefinable *je ne sais quoi* that drew her.

Perhaps it was his smile, the hesitant, slightly quirky twist to his lips, gone as swiftly as it had come; or perhaps the eyes, that strange combination of ice-blue and the dark, practically navy line around the iris that gave them a penetrating, almost haunting quality.

Whatever it was, Helen Cooper found his presence at the meeting distracting in the extreme.

His name, she learned, was Tom Russell, and he had just been offered the post of senior registrar to Ross Hamilton, one of the consultant general surgeons at the Audley Memorial.

Which meant of course, that she would be seeing very much more of him that was going to be good for her concentration, if today was anything to go by.

The meeting was an informal get-together, an opportunity for Tom to meet some of the team before he joined them at the beginning of May, and as they chatted over coffee Helen found her eyes straying to him again and again.

He was quieter than the rest — still, she imagined, on his best behaviour for the occasion — but his eyes followed the conversation and his mouth lifted now and again in response to a joke.

Oliver Henderson was there, propping up her desk and asking Tom if he had any ambition to be a cartoonist, which brought howls of laughter from the other members of the team and a puzzled frown from Tom.

Ross's smile was wry but good-natured. 'Ignore Oliver,' he told his new SR in his soft Scots burr. 'He's just trying to provoke me.'

A bleep squawked, and Ross's SHO, Gavin Jones, excused himself and lifted the phone. After a murmured conversation he turned to Ross.

'Sounds a bit tricky. They've got an RTA victim in the trauma unit—suspected leaky aorta.'

Ross set down his cup and stood up. 'Sorry, Tom, think this needs my attention. Sister Cooper will ply you with coffee and point you in the right direction, I have no doubt. I'll see you in a month—don't hesitate to ring if you've got any queries.'

They shook hands and Ross left with Gavin, followed by Oliver and then Linda Tucker, the staff nurse on duty, and Helen found herself alone with Tom in a silence that seemed to stretch on forever. Just when she thought she would have to find something to say to fill the void, he met her eyes.

'Do you mind if I ask you something?'

'No, of course not, ask away.'

'What was all that about cartoons?'

She laughed softly, caught off her guard. 'Oh—well, one of the surgical team was a bit of a joker. He's moved on now, but he's supplementing his hospital salary quite nicely by freelancing as a cartoonist for medical journals, I gather.'

Tom nodded, and the silence closed softly round them again, suffocating her. He seemed so close, so big, somehow, his hips propped against the windowill and his suit jacket drawn back by hands thrust casually into his trouser pockets in an unconsciously masculine gesture.

Awareness tingled through her, quickening her pulse and making her breathing unsteady. She looked away, taken aback by her reaction, and the silence yawned on. After a moment her natural good manners overcame her distraction.

'Would you like another cup of coffee?' she offered him, and was struck again by the haunting eyes.

'Thank you, but I'd better not. I've had about five cups already this morning—I'm in danger of drowning in it!'

His lips, firm but with a hint of fullness, quirked into an appealing smile and Helen felt her heart kick against her ribs.

'Another look round the ward?' she suggested, her composure really rattled now. They suddenly seemed very alone together in the little ward office.

'Have you got time?'

She laughed wryly. 'No, but the paperwork can wait.'

He laughed with her, a quiet, restrained laugh, and shrugged away from the window. 'If you're sure, then, I would appreciate it.'

He held the door for her, and as she passed through it she caught the faint trace of cologne, a subtle lemon fragrance tinged with something peculiarly masculine and very personal, something inextricably linked with her confusion and the strange, haunting feeling of being poised above an abyss.

And then he smiled, that strange, quicksilver smile, and she felt the edge of the precipice shift and start to crumble beneath her feet.

* * *

The first day back after the spring bank holiday was destined to be hectic from the start. Ross Hamilton's team were on take for emergencies, and Oliver Henderson had a list that morning. There were three day cases in for endoscopy and a fourth for sigmoidoscopy, and, if that wasn't enough, one of her staff nurses was off sick with a summer cold that had been doing the rounds.

Even so, and most untypically, Helen found time after she had taken the report and programmed her nurses to dive into the staff cloakroom and give herself a critical once-over.

Not, of course, that it had anything to do with a certain dark-haired, enigmatic young registrar who was starting work today—heavens, no!

But there was a becoming touch of colour in her pale cheeks, and deep in her soft grey eyes the light of hope glimmered. She didn't see that, of course. Instead she saw the mousy brown hair escaping from the bun, and the little smudge of mascara under her lashes—lack of practice, or a shaking hand? Could have been either, she thought, licking a tissue and dabbing at it. Better. She stood back and examined herself critically, tugging her uniform dress straight over her slight figure and staring, unsmiling, at her reflection.

What she saw dismayed her, and the ray of hope in her eyes flickered and died. With a sigh of resignation she turned away and went back to her duties with customary efficiency, putting aside her foolish fancies.

What would Tom Russell see in her, anyway? And besides, he was probably married, or at least engaged or living with someone. His type always were. It was only the perennial bachelors with the morals of alley-cats that were still free — and Helen wouldn't touch them with a barge pole.

Not that she was a prude exactly, but there was a line over which she wouldn't step, and casual sex with overgrown schoolboys fell far beyond that line.

So she was lonely, and a little out of practice at dating men, although she worked with them as patients and colleagues every day of her life without any problems.

No, he wouldn't be interested, and she was crazy to imagine he would be, she told herself firmly, and set about putting him out of her mind.

She was bent over a set of notes, transferring information on to the computer, when his voice sent a shock-wave through her.

'Any chance of that coffee you offered me a month ago?'

Schooling her expression, she straightened and turned.

'Dr Russell — welcome aboard.' Her words were stilted, but her smile was natural, open and generous, and her voice was filled with a warmth she was unable to disguise.

'Thank you,' he replied, his eyes searching hers, and his lips twitched briefly into that smile. 'Are you on my side?' he asked conspiratorially.

'Your side?' Helen was momentarily nonplussed.

'Yes — my side. Can I hide behind your skirts when I commit some bureaucratic misdemeanour and get yelled at by the powers that be?'

She chuckled. 'Is that likely?'

He shrugged. 'I hope not, but I must confess to a rotten case of nerves.'

'Oh, no we can't allow that!' she said with a smile. 'Come on.' She led him into her office. 'Here — coffee.'

There was a jug always on the go, at the insistence of the consultants who disdained the 'sewage produced by the canteen' and supplied their own coffee grounds. Helen poured Tom a cup and passed it to him, and then as he perched on the edge of the desk and downed it gratefully she watched him, unable to look away.

He was even more attractive than she had remembered, the smooth line of his jaw faintly shadowed even this early in the day. There was a tiny nick in the skin of his throat where he had cut himself shaving, and she wondered absently if anyone had kissed it better.

She looked away. Thoughts like that would get her nowhere. The cup rattled gently in the saucer, and she turned back.

'Gorgeous,' he said, his grin crooked. 'God, I needed that! Thank you.' He took a deep breath, then shrugged himself off the desk and smiled at her.

Her heart faltered for a second, then speeded up, much to her confusion. This was ridiculous! She couldn't react like this to him every time he smiled at her! She had to get things back on an even keel, and fast.

'How are you really feeling about starting here?' she asked him, determined to hold a normal conversation without blushing and stammering.

His grin was fleeting and hesitant. 'Really? I'm terrified,' he confessed.

'I don't believe you,' she told him bluntly. 'You don't look that easily intimidated.'

His eyes, those haunting ice and midnight-blue eyes, met hers and held, and they were backlit by a lurking glimmer of humour. 'I'm not usually. It must be first-night nerves — either that or a hang-over from last week's exams. I had the written papers for my FRCS Part Two, and I thought I was going to die of fright.'

'Unlikely,' she assured him drily. 'Still, I remember starting on this ward as sister. I was absolutely terrified, too, but everyone was so friendly. One of the older SENs came and perched on my desk and started to chat. I was so grateful to her, and it was fine after that — a lot of fun, in fact.'

His smile was wry. 'I doubt if it'll be fun.'

'Oh, I don't know. Ross Hamilton has a terrific sense of humour.'

'Hmm — I'll reserve judgement on that. I gather he's a hard task-master.'

She grinned. 'Only if you're totally incompetent — or if your name's Mitch Baker!'

His mouth quirked. 'Not guilty.'

Helen chuckled. 'Mitch was. He's the cartoonist I was telling you about. He drew an anonymous series of cartoons about Ross and Lizzi when they first started going out together, and some of them were a bit close to the knuckle. He probably would have got away with it if he'd been good at his job, but at that point he still had an awful lot to learn, and so, yes, Ross was hard on him, but he certainly deserved it, from what I can gather.'

'So,' he said, his eyes smiling, 'provided I'm whiter than white and toe the line, I'll be all right?'

'I don't think Ross would have taken you on if he hadn't thought highly of you,' she told him seriously. 'He doesn't suffer fools gladly.'

Tom sobered. 'That suits me,' he murmured,

'because neither do I. Right, what has he got for me this morning?'

'Four day cases, and you're on take for emergencies.'

'Fine. What are the day cases?'

'Two endoscopies for investigation of query gastric or duodenal ulcers, and an ERCP for query cholecystitis.'

He chuckled. 'The miracles of modern technology. Thank God for abbreviations — endoscopic retrograde cholangiopancreatography is a hell of a mouthful!'

'But probably quicker than saying sticking a tube with a camera on down someone's throat and into the duodenum and injecting radio-opaque medium into the bile duct to see what happens! Oh, and there's a sigmoidoscopy — middle-aged man with fresh blood in his stools — Ross is querying colitis or carcinoma; his wife reckons he's got piles.'

Tom looked thoughtful. 'Well, I hope to God she's the one that's right.' He glanced at his watch. 'Is it OK if I wait here? Hamilton said he'd meet me here at eight-thirty.'

Just then the door opened and Ross came in.

'Tom — good to see you again,' he said, extending his hand, and after a brief exchange of pleasantries he turned to Helen.

'Got the day cases in yet?'

'Yes — Gavin's clerked them and they've been prepped — they're all ready for you.'

'Good girl. Right, Tom, let's go and see you in action.'

'I can hardly wait,' he said drily under his breath, and winked at Helen, drawing his finger across his throat.

'Coward,' she muttered at his departing back, and he chuckled.

'Too damn right. Save me some coffee — I'll need it.'

And the door closed behind him, leaving her alone with her chaotic emotions.

They reappeared two hours later, deep in conversation and clearly troubled. Helen, back with her paperwork again, looked up, smiled and carried on.

'So what do you think we should tell him?' Ross asked, reaching for the coffee-pot.

'Hmm.' Tom propped himself against Helen's desk and shrugged. 'I don't know. What do you think the prognosis is?'

'I should say he doesn't have one,' Ross said candidly, passing Tom a cup of coffee. 'Helen?'

'No, thanks. Who are you talking about?'

'Ron Church — we've just done a sigmoidoscopy and he's got very widespread CA colon and rectum — God knows how he's been so symptom-free for so long.'

'Perhaps he hasn't,' Tom said quietly. 'Perhaps he just didn't realise it was anything to worry about till he started passing blood.'

'Yes, it's the fresh blood that frightens people. A higher bleed will usually go unnoticed. Oh, hell. So, what would you tell him?'

Tom frowned thoughtfully. 'That we found something that needs further investigation and removal? That he will have a colostomy, and that depending on what else we find he will need further surgery and possibly other treatment to alleviate symptoms. That it's possible that relieving pain and preventing further distress is all we will be able to do.'

Ross regarded him steadily. 'What if he says no?'

'Then he'll suffer unnecessarily, possibly intolerably.

I'd do my best to talk him into it, even if I know that we can't save him.'

'Would you mention the word cancer at this stage?'

'Maybe. I'd let him lead me on that.'

Ross nodded. 'Fine. Would you like to go and talk to him now?'

Tom looked resigned. 'If you think so, but I don't know him — wouldn't it be better if you gave him the news?'

Ross's mouth lifted in a wry smile. 'Now how did I know you'd say that?' he murmured, and, putting his cup down, he left the room.

'Poor chap.'

Tom looked at Helen quizzically. 'Who, Ross?'

Helen laughed. 'No, Mr Church. He seemed a nice man — he's only in his forties, isn't he?'

'Yes — forty-six. God, Helen, it was unbelievable considering his lack of symptoms. He's within a few days of perforating, I should say — if that.'

'His wife'll be shocked — she said this morning as she was leaving, "Oh, well, at least once they've done this you'll know there's nothing wrong and you'll be able to stop being such a worrywart." She'll feel dreadful, I should think.'

'I wonder,' Tom said slowly, 'if that's why he hasn't done anything until now? Although the bowel is notorious for not giving signals.'

'Yes.' Helen sighed. 'How about the others?'

'The endoscopies? Two duodenal ulcers and one narrow bile duct, probably due to scarring following an infection. No sign of any stones now, but Ross is going to operate and enlarge the duct if he can, and have a closer look. He might even link the gall bladder to the duodenum and bypass the bile duct — it looked pretty tight. We'll have another look at the plates before we operate, I guess, but I doubt we'll see anything new.'

'Are they staying?'

'Ron Church will be, I imagine, but the others will go out and come back in a few days or weeks — Mrs Tranter and her bile duct sooner, I suspect.'

Helen smiled teasingly at Tom. 'Funny how it's usually the men who get ulcers. It's because you all bury your emotions and won't talk to each other — everything piles up and becomes intolerable.'

A fleeting shadow crossed Tom's face, and he straightened up and set the cup down on her desk.

'Yes, very likely. Mind if I have a look at the post-ops?'

The sudden change in atmosphere was puzzling. What had she said? Had he taken her remarks as criticism? She hoped he wasn't going to be all tetchy and theatrical — it would drive her mad.

'Feel free,' she offered.

Then his bleep squawked and with a muttered, 'May I?' he reached for the phone.

She listened as he talked to the A and E department, and then he cradled the receiver and straightened up. 'Acute abdo in A and E — probably surgical.'

'Who did you speak to?'

'Chap called Jack Lawrence?'

'The consultant — if he says it's surgical, it's surgical. I'll get a bed ready. Once you've seen him, can you let me know if it's an ITU job?'

He grinned. 'Sure — and it's a she. Will you tell the boss?'

She nodded. 'You go on down — can you find the way?'

The grin widened slightly. 'Just about, I expect. I'll be in touch.'

She followed him out and with one of the junior nurses she prepared a bed for post-op in the side-ward nearest the nursing station where the patient could be observed continuously. Depending on the nature of the emergency, the patient would be specialled for the first few hours anyway if necessary, but a little extra supervision wouldn't go amiss.

She watched for Ross and saw him coming out of the little side-ward reserved for the day cases, his face grave. She followed him into her office and watched as he poured another cup of coffee. 'How is Mr Church?' she asked him.

'Unsurprised. He wants to tell his wife himself, and then I'll talk to her after he's seen her. Where's Tom?'

'He's gone down to A and E — acute abdo. I've alerted Theatre and prepared a bed. I'm just waiting to hear more.'

Just then the phone rang and she scooped it up. 'Surgical — oh, hello, Tom.'

'Hi — look, it's a woman, early twenties, looks like a burst appendix. Is Ross around?'

She handed the phone over, waited while Ross talked to Tom and then looked at him expectantly. 'Well?'

'I'll go in with him but I think Tom can handle it — he's very good, if his performance this morning is anything to go by.'

'So why go in?'

Ross shrugged. 'If it's a real mess it might take two of us to clean her up — and anyway, I'd like to see him in action.'

They were in Theatre for nearly two hours with her,

and when they came back to the ward Helen heard all about it.

'Ghastly mess,' Ross told her, reaching for the coffee. 'Must have been festering for months. Abcesses all over the place, all sorts of gynae implications — she's obviously had roaring pelvic inflammation for ages, poor kid.'

'What did you do?'

Tom pulled a face. 'What could we do? We cleaned her up as well as we could, repaired the damage and sewed her up again, but goodness knows how well she'll recover. She'll probably get an infective ileus, so don't assume that just because she's got bowel sounds she's ready for food, OK? It would just be the healthy bowel above the paralysed section trying to overcome the obstruction in the paralysed loops.'

Helen smiled slightly. 'Don't worry, Dr Russell — I'm well trained. I'll do nothing and give her nothing without instruction.'

Tom evidently picked up a slight reprimand because his face relaxed and he gave a rueful grin. 'Sorry — just making sure I didn't leave anything to chance. Oh, and one of the gynae chaps is coming down to look at her later. We took a vaginal swab and a smear test in Theatre just to be on the safe side before we started her on the IV antibiotics.'

'OK, I'll look out for him. Is she still in Recovery?'

Ross nodded. 'Yes, she'll be there for some time, I think.' He yawned hugely, and laughingly apologised. 'Sorry, Sarah was up in the night and Lizzi's feeling a bit rough at the moment so I ended up changing nappies and singing nursery rhymes at three o'clock.'

Helen chuckled. 'Do you good.'

He gave a non-commital grunt and helped himself to

more coffee, waving the pot at Helen and Tom, who both declined.

'You'll OD on that stuff if you aren't careful,' Helen remarked casually, and got a snort for her pains.

'*Et tu, Brute*?'

Helen grinned. 'Lizzi been nagging you?'

'Constantly. And I don't care if she is right.'

Tom looked at him thoughtfully. 'You look tired.'

'I am tired. I think I'm too old to be a father.'

Helen patted his prematurely grey hair teasingly. 'Poor old man — what a shame.'

He glared at her. 'Less of the old!'

'You started it!'

'Humph. Right, what's next?'

'Lunch?' she suggested.

He glanced at his watch and blinked. 'Lord, I suppose so — oh, well, we might as well grab something while we can. Coming, Tom?'

They left, and Helen went back out into the ward. Ruth Warnes, the staff nurse on duty, was standing at the nursing station staring after them.

'Wow,' she said, clearly awestruck. 'There aren't many like that around.'

Helen gave a non-commital shrug. 'Seems quite ordinary to me,' she lied.

Ruth eyed her suspiciously. 'Do you need your bumps felt? He's a dish!'

'Like tripe and onions,' Helen muttered.

Ruth chuckled. 'Philistine! I was thinking more of some exotic Eastern number full of fascinating spices and unusual combinations of flavours —'

'Now who needs their bumps felt?' Helen asked drily, and Ruth laughed.

'Never mind — no doubt he's on the menu for some

totally undeserving ingrate who doesn't appreciate the full subtlety of those wonderful blue eyes. . .' She sighed, and Helen felt an irrational urge to hit her. Instead she unlocked the drugs trolley from the wall and snapped her fingers under Ruth's nose.

'If I could drag you away from your reverie, Staff, perhaps you could spare the time to help me with the drugs?'

Helen went into the staff cloakroom, unpinned her frilly cap and tucked a wisp of hair back into her bun. She was feeling harrowed — harrowed and emotionally drained.

Ross had spoken to Mrs Church and explained the full implications of her husband's condition, and then left Helen to pick up the mess he left behind when he was called urgently to Theatre.

Tom stayed and talked to the Churches together once Mrs Church had settled down a little, and then Helen had given them a cup of tea and gone to see Judy Fulcher, the girl with the burst appendix who was down from Recovery.

She was doing reasonably well, nicely stable and not too nauseated, and Helen was happy that she was being nursed to her satisfaction. She had put Ruth on to special her as she had plenty of experience and was well aware of the implications of any possible change in her vital signs, but even so she had checked the chart herself, discussed her progress with Ruth and checked the flow of the drip and the suction drains from the stomach and the abdomen before she was happy to go off duty.

She was just coming out of the cloakroom when Tom walked through the double doors from the ward, his suit jacket slung over one shoulder, his car keys dangling from his hand.

'Hi — off now?' she asked him, and he nodded.

'Ross implied that I should get some sleep while the going's good — I think once I know where everything is and how it all works he'll chuck all the notes at me and run!'

Helen laughed softly. 'I doubt it, he's very conscientious. How are the Churches?'

Tom's face sobered. 'Pretty grim. Mrs is certainly taking it hard. I think actually he's known for ages that there was something pretty damn drastic wrong with him, so he isn't really surprised, but she is.'

'Yes, she seemed to be quite stunned. Is he going to have the op?'

Tom nodded. 'Yes, I think so. He's gone home for the night as planned, but I think he'll be back tomorrow for surgery.'

'Difficult start for you — I'm sorry.'

He threw her a quick grin. 'Doesn't matter when you start, Helen. It's always difficult for someone. I suppose that's why I'm here — to make it easier if I can't take it away. That's all any of us can do.' He glanced at his watch, then back at her. 'Got time for a cup of tea?'

'In the canteen?'

He wrinkled his nose. 'I was thinking of my room here — hospital tea is usually strong enough to stand a spoon up in, and I could do with something a little more subtle after all that coffee.'

She knew it was only a casual invitation and her reaction was probably foolish, but why not? She was tired and uptight, and anyway, she might find out something a little more personal about him.

'Tea would be lovely,' she said rashly.

They walked together through the sprawl of the hospital to the residents' wing, and he opened his door and ushered her in with a flourish.

'Welcome to Cell Block H.'

She looked round the small room, its cream walls chipped and bare, and chuckled. 'It is pretty basic, isn't it?'

His mouth quirked fleetingly. 'It's only temporary. I'm looking for something to buy—preferably something empty that I can move into quick! Park yourself if you can find anywhere.'

The only chair was stacked with books waiting to find a home, and a suitcase lay open on top of the chest of drawers.

Lacking any viable alternative, she sat on the end of the bed, her back against the wall, and watched him as he hung up his suit jacket on the back of the chair, tugged off his tie and rolled up his sleeves.

His jaw was deeply shadowed now, giving him a slightly rakish look and adding a dash of danger to an already very masculine man. Helen found it very unsettling, and she was deeply conscious of the nearness of his body and the intimacy of her surroundings.

Not that he did anything that could give her cause for concern—or at least not at first.

He plugged in a plastic jug kettle and flicked it on, then dropped on to the bed and shot her a grin. 'Mind if I change out of this suit? I've been suffocating all day.'

She shook her head, her mouth suddenly dry, and looked away as the zip rasped down and he peeled off the trousers.

'Now, the six-million-dollar question is, where are

my jeans?' he mumbled, and stood up to rummage through the suitcase.

She looked up and caught a glimpse of strong, straight thighs smothered in dark curls, so close that if she had lifted her hand she could have touched him. Her heart pounded and she felt the heavy, insistent beat of desire in her veins.

The threat was real now, close enough to touch, but it came, she realised, from within—which did nothing to diminish its impact on her starving senses.

Then his legs were plunged into battered old blue denim and he was turning towards her with a smile.

'Milk or lemon?'

'Oh.' Lord her mind had deserted her in those few brief seconds. 'Milk, please.'

He passed her a mug, and she cradled it in her hands and cast about for something sensible to say.

He spared her the trouble.

'How long have you been here?' he asked, propping himself up on the pillow and stretching his long legs down towards her—legs that were etched on her retinas and would trouble her sleep for weeks!

'Four years. I came to the hospital as a staff nurse on the other surgical ward, and when Lizzi stopped work to have the baby I got her job.'

Tom blew on his tea, took a sip and sighed with satisfaction. 'Better. So, are you happy here?'

'Oh, yes—very. It's a lovely hospital, and the staff are very friendly.'

'They are, aren't they? Ross seems really decent.'

'He is. So's Oliver Henderson. I'm very fortunate to be working with such reasonable people. The surgeon at my last hospital was a total pig.'

Tom chuckled. 'I've worked with a few of them.

Self-opinionated, over-blown stuffed shirts. Ross is a real breath of fresh air.' He looked at her oddly. 'And so are you.' His smile was brief, his eyes strangely intense. 'Thank you for making today so easy. I was dreading it.'

She was momentarily nonplussed. 'You — you're welcome,' she stumbled, and found herself wondering if there would ever come a time when she could see him smile without turning to mush inside.

CHAPTER TWO

HELEN didn't stay long. She found Tom's presence altogether too disturbing in that little room, and after finishing her tea she made some excuse and fled.

During the course of that night she spent a great deal of time telling herself that her reaction to him was fifty per cent imagination and fifty per cent the result of her solitary and loveless existence. By the morning she almost believed it, but ten minutes on duty threw a hefty spanner in those works.

She was just welcoming a very subdued Ron Church to the ward and beginning the process of admitting him when the hairs on the back of her neck stood up and Tom strolled into view, more casually dressed than the previous day in lightweight trousers and a white coat, and doing unspeakable things to her blood-pressure.

'Morning, Sister, morning, Mr Church,' he murmured, and with a fleeting smile he hitched one leg up and perched on the other side of the bed. 'How are you feeling today?' he asked the patient.

Mr Church sighed heavily. 'Resigned — scared, a bit.'

Tom nodded. 'Yes, it's all a bit of an unknown quantity, isn't it? Don't worry. Let Sister Cooper get all the paperwork out of the way and I'll come and have a long chat and see if I can set your mind at rest, all right?'

He moved away, going into the side-ward where Judy Fulcher had spent a fairly uncomfortable night following her burst appendix.

After Helen had finished with Mr Church she followed Tom in there and found him just covering Judy up again.

'That looks fine,' he said with a quick lift of his lips, and Judy gave him a wan smile in return.

'I feel awful,' she said.

'I'm sure. You've been brewing this for some time, though, so you're bound to feel rough for a few days until the antibiotics can get to grips with things. Still, you should be over the worst by now. We'll get you up later today and get you moving, and that should help to get you on the mend more quickly.'

She groaned with the thought, and Tom patted her hand. 'Don't worry, we'll take it very slowly. Just a few minutes in a chair at first, and then later perhaps a walk round the bed.'

They left the room, and he flashed a smile at Helen. 'Mr Church ready for me?'

She nodded. 'Yes, he is. He's very scared, Tom.'

'I'm sure. I would be, but then I know more than he does. I need to discuss him with you as well — perhaps we can do that first?'

She took him into the office and Tom explained that they were going to start by building him up a little. He would need blood transfusions to overcome the anaemia caused by prolonged blood loss from his ulcerated bowel before he would be fit enough for surgery. In the meantime he would be starved and his bowel emptied as far as possible to create as clean a field as they could for the operation.

Initially they would open him up to see if they could establish the extent of the tumour. Then they would remove as much as was necessary, depending on the progress of the growth. If it was too far advanced to hope for a cure, they would perform a palliative operation designed to minimise pain and distress in his remaining months. If they felt there was any hope of saving him, they would perform probably much more radical surgery including the removal of all of the descending colon, the rectum and anus and any affected lymph glands, in the hope that this more drastic approach would remove all the malignant cells.

Tom, however, was not optimistic.

'It looked too far gone, Helen. We'll do what we can, but——' He shook his head. 'Still, we can only try. Right, I'll go and have a chat to him.'

Tom's pessimism was well founded. When they finally opened Mr Church up on Thursday, they found the cancer had spread too far to hope for a cure, with metastases in the lymph nodes and invasion of surrounding organs, including his liver.

Ross felt that any surgical intervention should be aimed at causing as little distress as possible, and so they removed part of the descending colon and rectum and rejoined the ends, thus removing any immediate danger of obstruction and leaving the man his dignity for the short time he had left.

Tom found Helen after he came out of Theatre, and filled her in.

'What a damn shame,' she said sadly. 'He's such a nice man.'

'A least his wife will know what to expect,' he said enigmatically, and left her, puzzled, while he went to snatch some lunch before his clinic in the afternoon.

Ross came up during the afternoon and spoke to Mrs Church, and then Helen had the unenviable task of dealing with the shattered woman.

'I don't believe it,' she said over and over again. 'I

thought he had piles. I kept telling him not to make
such a fuss, and now it turns out he's dying!' She
pressed her fist against her mouth to stifle the sobs, but
to no avail. Helen put her arm round her and let her
cry, and after a few minutes she tried to pull herself
together. Helen gave her a cup of tea, and Mrs Church
was halfway through it before the tears got the better
of her again.

It was nearly five and time for Helen to hand over to
her staff nurse for the evening before Mrs Church
finally left, and as a consequence Helen had a mountain
of paperwork to wrestle with before she could leave.

She was just coming to the end of it when Ross and
Tom came in headed for the coffee-pot.

'How's Mr Church?'

'Asleep—he was very dopey. Ruth's specialling
him.'

Ross nodded. 'I'll pop in and have a chat before I go
home tonight, if he's awake enough. Otherwise I'll see
him in the morning. What about Judy Fulcher?'

'She's doing well—her peritonitis is settling and she
seems to be responding well to the antibiotics. Alex
Carter came and saw her yesterday and confirmed a
generalised gynae infection—he wants to keep an eye
on her. Seems she's got gonorrhoea, chlamydia and
candida among other things.'

Tom wrinkled his nose. 'Delightful. I thought she
was married?'

'She is,' Helen told them. 'Perhaps her husband
brought the bugs home?'

'How thoughtful,' Ross commented drily. 'Some
people have all the luck.'

Tom chuckled and put his cup down. 'Well, if it's all

the same to you I'm going to stick my nose in a book.
I've got my viva coming up altogether too quickly.'

'You'll walk it,' Ross said with a yawn. 'Oh, God,
I'm tired. Think I'll go home to bed. Oh, before you
go Tom, Lizzi and I are having a barbecue on
Saturday—all very informal, just a swim and a burger
in a bun. Lizzi ordered me to make sure you come.
She says it's high time she met you.'

Tom smiled slightly. 'Thank you, that would be
lovely. I'll look forward to it.'

Ross turned to Helen. 'What about you—any chance
you can make it?'

'Yes—super. Thanks, Ross.'

'I tell you what—why don't you come together?
Very ecologically sound—and there won't be so many
cars on my grass!'

Tom gave a short laugh. 'Fine—provided Helen
doesn't mind?'

She met his eyes—those strange, haunting blue
eyes—and thought of spending all that time alone in a
car with him. 'No—no, I don't mind,' she said quickly,
and her voice was slightly breathless, like an eager
girl's, she thought in disgust.

Ross shot her a keen look, but simply said, 'Good.
That's fine. Any time after three.'

Then she was alone, with the prospect of spending
Saturday afternoon and evening with Tom, and wondering what on earth she had let herself in for.

'Wow.'

Helen glanced across at Ross's house, sprawling
down the hillside like a Spanish villa, and then at Tom,
who looked faintly thunderstruck.

'It is a bit, isn't it? Look, park over there by those others under the trees.'

'Lord — a cast of thousands,' Tom said softly. He swung his Sierra off the drive on to the broad sweep of lawn that was covered in cars and pulled up beside a big dark grey Mercedes estate. 'I'm going to lower the tone a bit in this,' he joked, and tipped his head towards the Mercedes. 'Oliver's?' he asked.

She nodded. 'He's on call, but I guess his registrar will be doing it this afternoon.'

'Surprise, surprise,' Tom muttered under his breath. 'The joys of being a registrar.'

Helen chuckled. 'Poor old boy — you look really hard done by.'

He had the grace to laugh. 'Yes, I'm really badly treated, aren't I?'

'The trouble with Ross,' she told him as she gathered her things and climbed out of the car, 'is that he is incapable of delegating. That's why he's always so tired. He flings himself whole-heartedly into his job, and insists on doing the best for his patients. If that means he does the operation, so be it.'

Tom regarded her thoughtfully over the top of the car. 'But is it always the best for his patients? If he's tired, will he perform well?'

'The curse of the houseman. I think Ross perhaps hasn't realised that he's grown up!'

Tom chuckled. 'No, I think he feels the rest of us haven't — that's why he mothers and spoon-feeds us! Where do we go?'

'Follow the noise — and you're wrong, you know. He's been very complimentary about your operating — says you're good — and from Ross, believe me, that's high praise indeed.'

They strolled together across the grass and round the side of the house to the pool area, and Helen tried to ignore the long, lean, hair-strewn legs that ate up the ground so easily, and the snug fit of the tailored shorts that emphasised his narrow hips below the trim waist and wide, strong shoulders. She felt more than ever attracted to him, and was sure it must show in her eyes. She just wished she had the nerve to ask him if he was married or had a girlfriend, but she didn't really want to know. She might not get the answer she wanted, after all!

They turned the corner and Tom stopped in his tracks. 'Good God, I don't think I've ever seen so many babies out of a maternity unit!'

Helen laughed. 'Oh, well, they're all at it. There's Lizzi—come and meet her.'

They picked their way through the bodies strewn over the lawn to a slender, quietly pretty woman bent over a tiny toddler.

'Lizzi?'

She straightened, hitching the baby up on to her hip, and her face broke into a smile.

'Helen! I'm so glad you could come—and you must be Tom. Lovely to meet you. Welcome to the madhouse. Go and find yourselves a drink in the kitchen and come and have a chat.'

They made their way up the broad flight of steps leading to the house, and Tom shook his head slightly. 'Wow, again. What a house. I could almost forgive it for being modern, it does it so well!'

Helen chuckled. 'I take it you like old houses?'

'Oh, ideally, but I'm not having a lot of joy finding anything I like. Nothing lives up to the estate agent's blurb!'

They went into the house and found Ross in the kitchen piling burgers and sausages and chicken legs on to big plates. He was dressed only in a pair of scanty swimming-trunks, and looked disgustingly healthy and youthful.

'Just in time,' he told Tom with a grin, and handed him two of the plates. 'Take them down by the pool to the barbecue, and come back for the next lot. Right, Helen, what can I get you to drink? Hot, cold, with or without alcohol?'

'Cold without, please.'

'Fruit juice and fizzy water?'

'Lovely.'

He handed her the ice-cold glass and then carried on unwrapping food.

'Are you expecting an army?' she asked quizzically, eyeing the mountain of burgers.

'We've got the army already,' he said with a chuckle. 'Ah, Tom, well done. Help yourself to a drink.'

He pulled the ring on a can of beer and propped his hips against the worktop beside Helen, but Ross didn't let him linger.

'Go and enjoy yourselves,' they were told. 'Here, give that to Helen to carry and take this lot down to the barbecue on your way—oh, and could you tell Lizzi I could do with a hand with the salad?'

They found his wife sitting on the grass with her sleepy daughter on her lap, talking to Bron Henderson and Clare Barrington, both obviously pregnant.

Helen introduced them to Tom and gave Lizzi Ross's message, then Tom escaped to put the food down and talk to Oliver while Helen chatted to Bron and Clare.

'Lizzi looks tired,' Helen said thoughtfully, watching her as she made her way slowly up the steps.

'She is—this pregnancy's making her feel very sick and I think Sarah's giving them the run-around at night,' Bron commented with a wry laugh. 'Dear God, do I know the feeling! Jamie's being a holy terror at the moment, and heaven knows what it'll be like when this one comes along. Still, Livvy will be at school in September so it won't be so bad then.'

Helen grinned at Clare. 'Just think, you've got all this to look forward to!'

Clare chuckled. 'Yes, there are times when I think even sailing the Atlantic again couldn't be as bad as motherhood! Still, I wouldn't have it any other way.'

She looked across the pool to where Michael was standing talking to Oliver and Tom, and the loving expression on her face brought a lump to Helen's throat. How wonderful it must be to feel like that for someone and know it was returned, she thought wistfully, and found her eyes drawn to Tom.

He was laughing with the others, but at that moment he turned his head and caught her eye, and her heart turned over.

'He's gorgeous, isn't he?'

Helen turned back to Clare. 'Hmm?'

'Tom—he's gorgeous—if you like dark-haired men, which of course I don't!'

The girls all laughed, and Helen found her eyes drawn back to Tom again. Yes, he was gorgeous, but there was something else, some deeper quality that drew her against her better judgement.

She had found herself overpoweringly aware of him all week, almost to the point of being unable to concentrate on her job on occasions, and yet he had given her no hint that he returned her interest.

She sighed softly and turned back to the others,

determined to ignore Tom and get him out of her system.

'Sold the cottage yet?' Bron was asking, but Clare shook her head.

'No — we haven't really had time to think about it. Michael only started at Ipswich last weekend, and we've been too busy sorting things out to worry about putting it on the market. I suppose I'd better do that next week.'

Helen's interest was immediately caught. 'Look, I've got an idea. Tom's looking for a place, and I know he wants something old. Why don't you ask him if he'd like to see it?'

Clare looked across at him. 'Do you think he'd be interested?'

Helen shrugged. 'Might be. It wouldn't hurt to ask.'

Clare waved them over, and the three men strolled across.

'What's with the royal summons? Drinks run out or something?' Michael asked as they approached.

'No, no — Tom! Helen says you're looking for a house, and we've got a cottage to sell. It's only tiny, so it wouldn't be any use if you've got a wife and six children tucked away somewhere, but it is quite lovely, miles from anywhere and beautifully done up — '

'This is the soft sell, you notice,' Michael interrupted, and Clare blushed and giggled.

'Well, you know what I mean. It is lovely, Michael. I shall miss it.'

'No, you won't. My grandfather won't give you time to miss it, and once the bump comes along you certainly won't have time to mope. Anyway, Tom, as she says, the cottage isn't big, but you're more than welcome to have a look if you want.'

Tom nodded. 'Please. It sounds wonderful, and size isn't a problem, I'm on my own. When can I look at it?'

Clare and Michael exchanged glances. 'Tomorrow morning?'

'Fine. Can you give me directions?'

Helen saw Clare glance at her, then back to Tom. 'Why don't you get Helen to come with you? She knows the way, and it's a bit tricky to find the first time.'

'Helen?'

She met his eyes and shrugged. 'Fine. No problem.'

'Ten o'clock at the cottage?'

They all agreed, and then the conversation moved on, leaving Helen free to absorb Tom's admission that he was on his own. That didn't necessarily mean he was interested in her, of course, but it did mean he was free to pursue her if he wanted to. She would just have to wait and see if he did want to.

Lizzi joined them, followed by a trail of tiny children, with Ross bringing up the rear.

'It's like the National Childbirth Trust round here. Hoo-hoo-haaaah,' he huffed, and they all chuckled.

Tom looked quizzically at Helen.

'Breathing exercises for labour,' she told him, and he nodded blankly.

Ross chuckled. 'Not quite in your league, is it?' he said. 'Go and help yourselves to food—there's a stack of cooked bits and pieces, rolls, salad, et cetera. Eat plenty, for God's sake. There's always masses left over.'

Tom pulled Helen to her feet and they wandered over to the groaning table beside the barbecue.

'Oh, terrific—I'm starving!' Tom confessed, and

after they piled their plates up he led Helen away down
the garden to a little orchard at the end. Then he
lowered himself to the grass under the trees and patted
the ground. 'Sit down and tell me all about the
Barringtons' cottage.'

She settled herself beside him, taking a bite of her
burger to distract herself from the sight of his hair-
roughened thigh only inches from her knees. 'Well, it's
called Rose Cottage, and it's got roses climbing up it
and a thatched roof and little latticed windows, and it's
absolutely enchanting. If I could afford to, I'd buy it,
but I just don't earn enough.'

'Not fair, is it?' Tom said quietly. 'You work hard
enough, God knows. It's lovely to see you relaxing;
you've been rushing about all week. Every time I've
seen you you've been either bent over a patient or
buried under a mountain of paperwork.'

She sighed. 'Well, it's been a bit hectic. You've been
busy too.'

'Mmm. Still, I've enjoyed it. Thanks for all the help.'

She turned her head slightly and looked at him.
'You're welcome.'

His eyes locked with hers, and for an endless
moment they stared at each other, then he turned away
and bit into his roll, and she found she could breathe
again.

They ate in silence for a while, then Helen put her
plate down and lay back on the sweetly scented grass.

'Oh, heaven. I think I've eaten too much.'

'Rubbish. That's why you're so skinny. Do you want
the rest of this burger?'

She shook her head, and watched, fascinated, as
Tom picked it up and bit into it. His throat worked as

he swallowed, and she found the sight of his Adam's apple rising and falling absolutely riveting.

She made herself look away. Let him make the first move, she thought, and closed her eyes.

Seconds later his breath whispered against her cheek.

'You've caught the sun,' he said softly, and his finger trailed down her nose.

'Freckles,' she said unnecessarily, and he counted them.

'Fifteen.'

'Are you sure? There were twelve this morning.'

He chuckled softly. 'Is that a fact? I told you you'd caught the sun.'

She opened her eyes and found herself staring straight into his, just bare inches from her face. Her lips parted involuntarily on his name, and for an endless moment she thought he was going to kiss her.

Then he rolled away and stood up. 'I'm going for a dip — coming?'

'You shouldn't swim so soon after eating,' she told him mechanically.

'Tough,' he replied, and there was an edge of hardness in his voice she hadn't heard before.

She watched him walk away, his long legs eating up the grass in great strides, and wondered what she'd done wrong.

He fell in love with the Barringtons' cottage on the spot, and Helen strolled round the pretty garden while they agreed a price and decided on a completion date. He had apparently sold his house in Oxford to a cash buyer, and was able to go ahead as quickly as Clare and Michael were willing to.

Helen was very pleased for them all. Tom was so

clearly thrilled with the cottage, and on the way home afterwards he positively bubbled with enthusiasm. It was the most animated she had ever seen him, and Helen was secretly delighted. He looked so sad for much of the time, and to see him like this, brimming over with excitement and plans, was a real joy.

It was also infectious, and she found herself laughing as she hadn't laughed in ages.

And then suddenly, without warning, his mood changed again.

Afterwards she found it difficult to put her finger on exactly what had happened. They were talking about when he was to move in, and he said he'd have to buy furniture. Then she asked how come he'd owned a house and didn't have any furniture, and that was when he went funny.

'It was all borrowed,' he said shortly, 'and anyway, it's time for a change.'

And after that he hardly said a word all the way back, and dropped her off outside her flat without even a smile. She was bitterly disappointed, because they had been getting on so well and she'd hoped he would suggest they go somewhere for lunch together — instead of which he had driven off with a stony face and left her alone again.

She let herself into her flat and made a sandwich, then sat by the window looking out into the concrete back yard, relieved only by a sorry-looking lilac that struggled for existence in a crack in the paving.

It was such a contrast to Rose Cottage and Ross's house that she indulged in a moment of self-pity before changing into tatty old jeans and a T-shirt and picking up the keys of her sensible, middle-of-the-road little car.

'God, I'm so *bored*!' she said savagely as she banged the door of the car. 'Bored, bored, bored, bored, *bored*!'

She headed out into the country and found herself in a little village with a winding stream that gurgled under an old brick bridge. Parking the car in a lay-by, she locked it and set off on a hike along the stream.

It was a gorgeous day — a day to share, she thought crossly, and felt suddenly very lonely and sad.

'There was no guarantee he felt anything for you,' she told herself firmly as she walked. 'He's just as entitled to be as picky as you are — and he's obviously decided not to pick you. God knows he gave you enough warning — he was hardly all over you. And yesterday — he could have kissed you so easily, but he didn't. And still you expect miracles!'

'Pardon?'

She looked up, startled, to find a woman with a dog regarding her strangely.

'Are you all right, dear?'

She blushed and laughed. 'Sorry — yes, I'm fine. I was just telling myself off.'

'On a lovely day like this? What a shame.' The woman smiled, and Helen smiled back, suddenly happier.

'Yes, you're right. It's much too nice a day to be cross.'

They parted company, the woman and her dog going on the way Helen had come, Helen following the track beside the stream.

She was right, it was a beautiful day, and being cross and ungracious was just a waste of it. She would put Tom out of her mind, and forget him.

Easier said than done, she acknowledged the following morning.

How he had managed it in so short a time she didn't know, but Tom Russell had winkled his way into her heart in a big way, and it would take more than a little determination to get him out again.

He was quiet and withdrawn when she saw him, but they were so busy that she hardly had time to chat anyway.

Judy Fulcher, the patient with the burst appendix and peritonitis, was making slow but steady progress, althought she was still unable to take anything by mouth. As a result oral care was a very important part of her nursing, and Helen took the opportunity, to sponge off her caked lips and tongue and clean her teeth as a training exercise for Carol, one of the student nurses who had started with her that day.

Judy's gratitude was touching, and Helen wished she had time to do it better and more often.

However she didn't, and she was busy with the pre-ops who were due to go up to Tom in Theatre that afternoon.

Trailing her students, she prepared the patients for Theatre, including passing a Ryle's tube into one man who found the whole experience intolerable and panicked himself into a frenzy.

'Look, Mr Blackstone,' she explained for the second time, 'it really doesn't hurt. All you have to do is relax as much as possible, take little sips of water and swallow gently, and I'll just slip the tube down your throat bit by bit. It's really not that bad.'

He snorted and put his hand over his face. 'I'm not having no bloody tube poked down my throat!' he mumbled.

'Please let me try,' she coaxed. After a few more minutes he lowered his hand, and, taking the lubricated tube, she lifted it towards his nose.

'No,' he moaned, and covered his face again.

Tom arrived just as she was soothing the man down for the third time, and with his help she managed to calm him sufficiently to try again.

This time she actually succeeded, much to her relief, and afterwards, when the tube was taped in place and the man's stomach had been aspirated and he was settled, Tom drew Helen aside.

'You were wonderful with him,' he said gently, and the sun came out for her again.

Foolish heart, she chided herself, and tugged off her gloves. Her smile was coolly impersonal.

'He's just a big baby. What can I do for you?'

He sighed quietly. 'Could we go round the pre-ops? Do you have time? I wanted a last word with them.'

Her heart sank. She had thought—oh, never mind what she had thought. She forced another smile. 'Of course. Susan, clear up the trolley could you, please? And then start the lunches. Carol can give you a hand. Oh, and Susan?'

'Don't forget to read the menu list,' the third-year student said with a grin. 'OK, Sister.'

Helen watched her go. 'Scatty as the day is long, but willing. Right, where were we?'

The rest of the day was hectic, and that suited Helen just fine, because the last thing she needed was time to think about Tom. She felt she had come within an ace of making a complete fool of herself over him, and he so clearly wasn't interested.

Oh, well.

She was just going off duty at five when she heard a commotion in Judy Fulcher's room.

The door was shut, most unusually, and when she opened it she saw to her horror that Judy's husband was sprawled across the bed, his trousers round his ankles, and Judy was sobbing and pleading with him as he dragged her nightdress up.

For a second Helen was so stunned she did nothing, but then she leant on the bell over the bed and seized his shoulders.

He shrugged her off, and she stumbled back, steadying herself on the locker.

'What on earth do you think you're doing?' she asked furiously, and grabbed hold of him again, determined to drag him off. He flung her aside and she landed on the floor with a crash, shaken but not seriously hurt. She was more worried about Judy, still struggling with her half-crazed husband.

As she crawled to the door for help, so Tom appeared in the doorway and with one look at the scene stepped over her and hauled the man off, slamming him up against the wall.

'What the bloody hell do you think you're playing at?' he roared. 'She's ill, for God's sake!'

'She's always ill!' he snarled. 'Always got some damn excuse or other. I've got rights, you know, and I haven't had it for months!'

'What about *her* rights?' Tom yelled into his face. 'What kind of an animal are you that she's lying there after a major abdominal operation and all you can think about is getting your leg over?'

Helen tried not to smile. Tom was so furious with the man it would be a miracle if the latter survived intact!

She stood up, dusted herself down and went to make sure that Judy was all right.

Ruth Warnes had heard the bell and come to help, and between them they settled Judy down again and made sure her drip hadn't become dislodged, while Tom hauled up the man's trousers with more vigour than was strictly necessary and dragged him off to the office.

Judy was crying, and Helen left Ruth comforting her and went to phone the hospital security. Just as she got through there was a crash from her office, and she put the phone down after begging the security officer to hurry and ran into the office, to find Mr Fulcher pinned to the floor, Tom with blood running down his face and glass everywhere.

'Security's coming,' she said briefly, and Tom nodded.

'Fine. Just so long as they're quick, before I'm tempted to run this bloke through with a scalpel.'

'He threatened me!' Fulcher mumbled against the floor. 'Did you hear that? Threatened me, he did.'

'I shouldn't let it worry you,' Helen said drily, eyeing Tom's bleeding eyebrow. 'He's the one running with blood. Are you going to press charges, Tom?'

'If I don't bleed to death first,' he muttered. 'Where the hell are they?'

Just then the security staff came running in and Tom stood up, handing his charge over to the uniformed officials.

'Lock him up till the police get here,' he said shortly.

'Right, sir,' one of them muttered, and then they hauled the man to his feet and marched him out of the office.

Helen shut the door and turned to Tom. He was

pale, trembling slightly with reaction, and the cut over his eye was still welling blood.

'You look awful—sit down and let me look at that.'

He tipped the broken glass off the chair and sat down obediently, tipping his head back so that she could examine the cut.

'What on earth did he hit you with?' she asked incredulously.

'The coffee-jug—ouch!'

'Sorry. It's a good job it was empty.' She probed again, and he flinched. 'There's a bit of glass left in there, and it'll need a stitch. Do you want to go down to A and E?'

He peered up at her from under his eyebrows. 'Can't you do it?'

She looked doubtful. 'I can, but—I might leave a scar.'

'Shame,' he said softly. 'Just stitch it, Helen.'

She took him into the treatment-room and made him get on the couch.

'Don't bother with the lignocaine,' he told her as she picked up the syringe. 'If it's only one stitch it'll hurt less just to do it.'

She shrugged and washed her hands, then opened the suture pack, swabs and antiseptic before pulling on gloves. It was his head, she reasoned. If he wanted it stitched without a local, so be it. And anyway, he was probably right, a local anaesthetic did hurt.

She lifted out the glass and swabbed the cut with antiseptic, and he winced and flinched.

'Sorry—that's probably the worst bit.'

'God, I hope so,' he said with a weak attempt at humour. 'It brings the tears to your eyes.'

'Just tough it out, cowboy,' she told him firmly. 'You wanted it this way — OK, hang on, here it comes.'

He didn't move a millimetre, but she could see the muscle jumping in his jaw and knew it was hurting him.

'OK, all done,' she said seconds later, and snipped the suture.

He sagged back against the couch and shot her a weak smile. 'Thanks.'

'My pleasure.'

'Sadist.'

She snorted and wiped the skin around the cut dry before putting on a couple of butterfly sutures each side of the stitch. 'It was your idea to play the hero,' she told him laughingly.

'Hmm. Remind me next time not to bother,' he said with a smile, and her stupid heart went into overdrive again.

She turned away, clearing up the debris from her suturing, and he was so quiet she thought he'd fallen asleep. Then his hand rested lightly on her arm and turned her towards him.

'About yesterday. . .'

She forced herself to meet his eyes.

'What about it?'

'I'm sorry I got ratty. It's just — the furniture was a bit of an issue in the past. You just hit a nerve. I'm sorry I was short with you.'

All the lectures she had given herself over the past twenty-four hours went out of the window at a stroke. She knew the smile must have lit up her eyes, but there was nothing she could do about it.

'Forget it,' she told him. 'I thought it must be something I'd said or done to irritate you — '

'No. No, Helen, it was nothing to do with you. You've been marvellous.'

He sat up and swung his legs over the side, and his mouth quirked into that fleeting smile again.

'Forgive me?'

'Of course I forgive you,' she said softly, and wondered if her heart would stand the strain of that wretched smile.

CHAPTER THREE

THE police came and interviewed Tom and Helen, and then talked to Judy Fulcher who was still very shaken but clearly so familiar with the pattern of her husband's behaviour that she was unsurprised.

The only surprising thing, she told Helen, was that he had waited so long. However, even under pressure from the police she refused to press charges.

'If he goes to prison, he'll kill me when he gets out,' she explained, and behind her matter-of-fact delivery Helen sensed a deep-rooted terror.

Instead of going off duty as she had planned, Helen sat and talked to Judy, letting her pour out all her troubles, and gradually a picture built up of a long-term pattern of abuse, both physical and mental, that had turned Judy into the submissive, diffident woman that Helen had been nursing for the past week.

Helen promised her that the medical social worker would come and talk to her in the morning, and that if she didn't want to return to her husband she wouldn't need to.

Again, Judy felt that there was no way she could escape from him, that if she left him he would find her and kill her.

'It's not that he's deliberately cruel,' she explained. 'It's just that he's got definite ideas, and if I agree with him that's fine, but if I want anything different — like this sex thing. I've been feeling awful for months, but still he insisted. When I finally told him I couldn't stand

46

it any more, he started going off with other women—prostitutes, mainly. So I let him do it with me after that—well, people were talking. Anyway, it's hardly the first time.'

Helen didn't know what to say, but it didn't matter. Now she had started, Judy talked for hours, and it was nearly ten o'clock before she felt able to leave her.

She went into the sister's office and found Tom, slouched in a chair, reading a weighty textbook.

'You're still here!' she said, surprised.

He put the book down and smiled fleetingly. 'I was waiting for you. I went and got a book—it looked like a long job.'

Helen nodded and sank into the other chair. 'Yes. God, what a coil, Tom. That man is a complete bastard.'

Tom gave a wry chuckle. 'Tell me about it! I've got a hole in my head that says so.'

She looked at the cut, now swelling and colouring well, and shook her head. 'It looks sore.'

'Surprise, surprise,' he murmured. 'Are you OK, by the way? I gather he threw you on the floor.'

She shrugged. 'Bit sore here and there—I landed on my tail.'

'Ouch. I'd offer to kiss it better but it's a bit public.'

She stared at him blankly for a second, then started to laugh, the reaction of the past few hours finally surfacing. When the laughter turned to tears she didn't know, but she found herself in Tom's arms, her head cradled against his chest, his voice soft and soothing in her ear.

It felt wonderful, and she wanted to stay there forever, but common sense asserted itself and she pushed him gently away.

'Here.' He put a tissue in her hand and she blew her nose and wiped her cheeks, then gave him a tremulous smile.

'Sorry.'

'His eyes were warm and filled with understanding. 'Don't apologise. It's all been a bit much. What did she say?'

So Helen filled him in, telling him all the sordid and depressing facts of Judy's existence with her bully of a husband.

'She said that in the end she let him do it with her— Tom, it should be an act of love, not some kind of barely tolerable sacrifice!'

With exquisite gentleness, Tom took her face in his hands and smoothed his thumbs over her damp cheeks.

'Shh. We'll get her some help, Helen. Don't fret— there's nothing you can do tonight. The police have got him cooling his heels in a cell and won't let him go till the morning, so she's quite safe.'

His eyes tracked slowly over her face, lingering on her mouth, and then with a quiet sigh he let her go, turning away and picking up his book. 'If you're sure you're OK, I'll go and turn in. I've got to finish this before the morning.' He hefted the book in his hand, and with a wry grin he opened the door, winked at her and left.

She sat down again, her legs suddenly weak. That was the second time he had almost kissed her and then pulled away. The first time, under the trees at Ross's barbecue, she had thought it was because she had engineered the situation a little and he hadn't wanted to kiss her. This time, she was sure he had wanted to and for some reason had pulled himself away.

Perhaps she was right. Perhaps he had a girlfriend

somewhere that he was still seeing—or maybe it had been her furniture and that was why he had got so uptight yesterday. Whatever, he was clearly not about to take their relationship any further. The fact that he apparently wanted to was cold comfort indeed.

'Ron Church had to go to Theatre in the middle of the night,' Jean Hobbs, the night sister, told Helen when she came on duty at eight. 'Femoral embolus. Tom Russell opened the artery and removed the clot, and he's on a Heparin drip now and reasonably comfortable. We're watching him for any sign of further clotting, but Tom said it seemed pretty self-contained and he's hopeful he got it all.'

'Oh, poor man. You'd think he'd got enough to contend with without this.'

Jean gave a wry smile. 'Are you talking about Mr Church, or Tom Russell?'

Helen laughed. 'I meant Mr Church, but I suppose it applies to Tom, too. Any other developments?'

'Judy Fulcher's OK after last night's fiasco—oh, Tom's got a cracker of a black eye, by the way. That was a lovely suture you put in.'

'That's a miracle. He should have had two, really, but he refused a local, and I had to force myself to do one!'

'Wow, what a hero!' Jean said laughingly. 'I have a jab at the dentist for a scrape and polish!'

Helen chuckled. 'Yes, well, I think he regretted it. So, what else has been going on?'

Jean stared at her in disbelief. 'You want more?'

'Just the run of the mill, Jean.'

'Right. Well, Mrs Tranter is in for her bile duct investigation tomorrow—she's had a comfortable night but she's a bit nervous. There was quite a lot of kerfuffle with Ron Church and I think it unsettled her a bit. Oliver's patients all slept well; they've been prepped and they're all ready for their pre-meds. Oh, and that man who had his GU done yesterday — Mr Blackstone. He was groaning a bit in the night, but I think he's all right. We kept an eye on him. I think he just doesn't cope very well with discomfort.'

'No, well, he didn't cope very well with the Ryle's tube either. I thought at one point I was going to have to hold him down and ram it down his throat!'

'Helen!'

She chuckled. 'Only joking. I sweet-talked him in the end with Tom's help. I'll go and have a chat with him, find out how he is this morning. Is that the lot?'

'Yup. Right, I'm off for supper. Byesy-bye.'

'Bye, Jean. Thanks.'

Helen took the keys from Jean as she left and after glancing through the print-out she went out into the ward, going first to the nursing station.

'Right, Linda, could you special Ron Church for me this morning? He had a femoral embolus in the night —— Oh, and have a look at Judy, could you? I'll go and see her later when I've got a minute, but I've got to get these pre-meds done with Ruth first.'

The staff nurses organised and the rostered third-year students dispatched about their duties, Helen took Ruth Warnes and the second-year student to do the pre-med drugs for the patients on Oliver Henderson's morning list.

It was a busy morning, and it was after the ten o'clock drugs round before she had time to go in to Judy. She learned that the social worker had already been in, and that arrangements had been made for a court order forbidding Judy's husband to come to the hospital again until further notice.

Judy was unconvinced, but Helen managed to assure her that the security services would be on the look-out for him and she would be quite safe.

She also moved her out into the main ward, since she felt it would be safer for her, and moved Ron Church into the little room where she could keep a closer eye on him and where he would be quieter.

He was drowsy but philosophical.

'Thought my number was up,' he told her. 'That young man won't give up on me, will he? Pity I didn't go, really—save everybody a lot of trouble.'

She perched carefully on the edge of the bed and took his hand in hers. 'Don't say that—you're no trouble, that's what we're here for. Once we get you over this, you'll soon be up and around again, and hopefully we'll be able to keep you quite fit and pain-free for quite some time.'

He looked away. 'I had an aunt who went into one of those hospice places—she loved it there. Went to visit her once, and I must say it was very nice, but I never thought for a moment I might be needing it myself soon.'

'Not for a while, Ron. There's life in you yet.'

He gave her a wry smile. 'Yes, I suppose so. At least I can still tell a pretty girl when I see one, eh?'

He squeezed her hand gently, and she flushed self-consciously and gave an embarrassed little laugh. 'Don't be silly.'

'Not being silly, am I, Doc? She a lovely little thing.'

Helen looked up to find Tom, his eye swollen and discoloured, regarding her with a strange expression on his face. 'Yes—yes, she is, Ron. Very lovely.' He continued to look at her for a second, then seemed to collect himself and turned his attention to his patient.

'How are you this morning? Feeling better?'

'Bit sore, but better than I was, thank you.'

'He's being a martyr,' Helen told Tom. 'Says he should have gone last night and saved us all the trouble. I'll leave you to talk some sense into him.'

She stood up, shot Mr Church a grin and escaped, her mind reeling. Was he just being gallant, or did Tom really think she was very lovely? If so, he needed his head examined, she thought philosophically, and busied herself with one of Oliver's patients back from Theatre.

The second-year student nurse who had just started her two-week placement with Helen proved very well based in theory but very nervous in practice. She reminded Helen a lot of herself in her first ward placement, except that when she trained she had spent eight weeks in PTS, not something over a year in a mixture of theory and practical observation. Carol, the student, felt she knew very little. Helen, on the other hand, had known far less on her first ward and been charged with terrifying responsibility. She knew which was the better system—provided the students didn't come on to the ward full of their own knowledge and training and pile in headlong out of their depth, as sometimes happened.

She took Carol through the post-op routine, including the little wash and freshen-up which patients usually appreciated provided it was fairly superficial and not too invasive.

'What they don't need,' she told Carol, 'is hauling about and washing in every last nook and cranny. Just a quick once-over with a warm flannel and they settle back to sleep very quickly. It's also a subtle way to check the drain is working well and the wound looks stable — OK?'

Carol nodded.

'Good. Fine. You can do the next one.'

'What?'

Helen grinned at her. 'Don't panic, I'll be here. You've got to start somewhere. Just take it nice and steady, and be gentle, and don't forget to talk to the patient.'

By the time they had finished, the next patient was back and Carol was much more confident and able to carry out the whole procedure competently and without any help.

'Well done,' Helen told her afterwards, and then sent her off to lunch.

Tom found her in the office. 'How's your tail?' he asked.

She laughed softly. 'Fine, thanks. How's your eye?'

'Colourful. I knew that coffee-pot was bad news, but I never for a moment realised why!'

That smile again. She moved a little closer and inspected the stitch. 'It looks quite good, really. I doubt if you'll have a visible scar, because it follows the lines on your brow.'

He glowered at her. 'Are you accusing me of having wrinkles?'

She giggled. 'God forbid — it would wreck your heroic image. No, not wrinkles, Tom — character lines.'

'Character lines!' he said in disgust. 'I'm not even thirty-two yet, and she's giving me character lines!'

'Ah, well, you have to be young, otherwise they *are* wrinkles!' she teased.

'Like Ross, growing into his prematurely grey hair.'

'Exactly. Now he's forty he's running out of excuses—he's just plain grey!'

'You talking about me?' Ross growled from behind her, and she jumped and giggled.

'Me? Would I?'

'Plain, indeed—I'm offended.'

Tom gave a rueful grin. 'We were discussing how my wrinkles will disguise my scar.'

Ross chuckled. 'Better as time goes by. That reminds me—you, young man, owe me a coffee-pot. I had to go down to the canteen and drink slop this morning. Filthy stuff—it took years off my life!'

'You should have gone to A and E and had some of Jack Lawrence's coffee,' Helen told him.

'Good idea. I'd forgotten about that.' Ross squinted at Tom's eyebrow and pursed his lips thoughtfully. 'Nice bit of needlework, Helen. Well done.'

'Thanks. Oh, by the way, I've moved Judy into the main bay for her own safety.'

'Good idea,' Ross agreed. 'Right, we've got Mrs Tranter in for her bile duct op—I just want to have a look at the X-rays again.'

Helen found the plates and switched on the light box, and they stood back and studied the plates one by one while Ross described what he intended to do. He was just about to turn off the light when Tom stopped him.

'What's this?'

He was pointing at an area of her spine and pelvis on the bottom of the plate, and, when they looked carefully, tiny white spots were visible, scattered over the ilia and up the spine.

'God knows,' Ross muttered grimly, and put the other plates up again.

'Metastasis?' Helen murmured.

'Looks very like it—well, where the hell from? Where's her primary tumour?'

Tom and Ross looked at each other, then back at the plates.

'Nothing to do with her liver or gall bladder,' Ross said thoughtfully. 'Has she got any breast history?'

Tom flicked through her notes and shook his head. 'None recorded here that I can see, and her records go back to 1978.'

'Well, damn.' Ross reached absently for the coffee-pot, and swore softly. 'Helen, could you rustle up a couple of cups of instant? Tom, give me those notes. I'd stake my life on it being breast or ovarian—that's a typical hormonal scatter of metastases——'

Helen went into the kitchen and made a jug of instant coffee and a few cheese sandwiches, then took the tray back in. Ross was on the phone to the radiologist, arranging an MRI scan. He put the phone down and turned back, thanking Helen absently and munching a sandwich as he glared at the X-rays.

'Helen, I want to have a look at her, but I don't want to alarm her at this stage. She's already twitchy, from what I can gather. Got any ideas?'

'Chest exam for the anaesthetic?'

'Stephen will come down and do that himself shortly, though.'

'Not if you stop him,' Helen pointed out.

'OK. Right, come on, then. You coming, Tom?'

He shook his head. 'No, I don't think so. The fewer there are of us, the less nervous she'll be. I'll stay here and eat sandwiches.'

So Helen went with Ross and helped Mrs Tranter undress so that Ross could examine her, and after he had finished he told her there were one or two other X-ray-type procedures they wanted before she went to Theatre in the morning.

'No nasty tubes like the last time,' he reassured her, and she smiled in relief.

'Oh, good, I didn't like that at all!'

Ross patted her hand and stood up, and Helen tidied her up and followed him back to the office.

'Left breast,' she said economically, and he nodded.

'The skin's tighter, and her left nipple is a fraction higher. Her left arm's also slightly swollen, so it's in the lymph nodes. Blast.'

'Still going for the MRI?' Tom asked.

'Have to—find out where else it is. And the oncologist could do with a ring once we've got something more definite for him.' He glanced at the empty plate and then at Tom, who grinned.

'Sorry. I was hungry.'

Helen sighed in resignation and went back to the kitchen to make some more sandwiches for Ross, and on the way back she glanced into Ron Church's room.

He was lying propped up on his pillows, a book on his lap, and he waved at her and winked. She smiled and waved back, then went into the office.

Ross and Tom were still discussing Mrs Tranter, so she carried on with the endless ward paperchase that dogged her existence while Ross mucnhed the sandwiches and muttered about possible treatment and outcome.

She was just going back to the ward when a bell rang. By the time she was through the door she found Ruth and Carol at Mr Church's bedside, and Ruth was yanking out the pillows and rolling him on to his back.

'He's arrested,' she said economically, and Helen

dispatched Carol to fetch Ross and Tom, and grabbed the resus trolley from the nursing station.

Ross appeared and went smoothly into action, but Tom stood on the threshold, his face set.

'Why don't you let him go?' he asked.

Ross stopped what he was doing and slowly straightened.

'You think we should?'

Tom's face could have been cast in stone. 'Yes, I do. He was ready. What are you saving him for? To die again? Just because your heart's beating doesn't mean you're alive.'

Helen stopped what she was doing and looked harder at him, and the bleakness in his eyes chilled her to the bone.

'I think he's right,' she said after a second. 'I think there's a time to let go, and I think this is it.'

Ross nodded. 'OK. I doubt if we could have got him back, but if we had, what for, as you said? To suffer for another few months and then go anyway?' He sighed heavily. 'OK, clear up in here, could you, and I'll go and write up his notes? Oh, and someone needs to look out for his wife. She'll be in this afternoon.'

Helen removed all the tubes and drains from Mr Church's body, then covered him with the sheet and led Carol, pale and shaking, away.

'I'm sorry you had to get involved in that,' she said quietly.

'That's why I'm here, isn't it?' Carol gave a ragged sigh. 'He just looked so cheerful earlier. He was all smiles and jokes.'

'He waved to me,' Helen said pensively, 'just minutes before, when I was passing the door. He looked fine.'

'His poor wife.'

Helen shrugged. 'Believe me, it's a terrible shock whenever it happens, no matter how much warning you've had. At least this way he didn't have to suffer too much. Right, I've got a nice little job for you — you've got to take Mrs Tranter down to Radiology for a scan. You'll find a wheelchair just outside the door, and she'll need a blanket over her legs. The corridors can get very chilly. Oh, and get her notes from me on the way, then come back and help me do the drugs with Ruth.'

She was deliberately keeping the girl busy, and she wished someone would have the foresight to do it with her, because all she could see was the agony on Tom's face, and the despair in his eyes.

Mrs Tranter had a primary tumour in her left breast, which had invaded the lymph glands under her arm and also spread into the chest wall. On balance it was decided that she should have radiotherapy for the breast area and the skeletal metastases, and her bile duct operation would proceed as planned as there was now some concern that the narrowing could be due to pressure from another, secondary tumour, perhaps in the pancreas.

In fact it wasn't, but Ross was able to eliminate any fears of liver involvement at the same time as he widened the duct by releasing scar tissue that had built up around it following previous bouts of infection. He removed her gall bladder as a precaution, and then sent her back to Helen for after-care — not something Helen relished, because Mrs Tranter had managed to work herself up into a frenzy following Ron Church's' death, and was now convinced she was about to die post-operatively and without warning.

She wasn't the only one affected by Ron's sudden death. Tom, too, was quiet and withdrawn, and Helen found that she was totally unable to read him any more.

Whereas on that day his face had been filled with emotion, now it was almost totally expressionless, only the eyes giving away any inner demons.

Helen ached for him, and longed to ask what was wrong. He was too distant, though, and she felt it was impossible to come out cold and just say, What's the matter? Why are you hurting?

Ross, too, noticed the change in him and commented on it to Helen.

'I wonder what it is?' she said thoughtfully.

'Could be just hard work. He's got his viva coming up in a couple of weeks—maybe he's panicking.'

She shrugged. 'Maybe.' But she felt it was more than that, and towards the end of the week she decided to brave his wrath, and went and knocked on his door in the residence.

'He's out,' she was told by one of his neighbours. 'Came down from Theatre, changed and went about five o'clock. I doubt if he'll be back till late; he isn't usually.'

And Helen, who thought he spent every evening studying, found another piece of the jigsaw was missing.

The next day, Friday, he was more his usual self, and Helen was too busy to worry about him anyway.

Mrs Tranter, having been given the news of her breast cancer and secondaries by Ross and the oncologist who would be taking over her care, needed a great deal of support and understanding, and at the other end of the spectrum Mr Blackstone with his gastric ulcer repair was being a total pain.

'That man is a wimp!' Helen declared to Ruth after she had done the drugs round and refused to give him an excess of pain-killers. 'I don't wonder he got an ulcer—he's such a worrywart! "This hurts—that's uncomfortable—could you just move this—fetch that—give me the other?" Aggh! I could scream!'

Tom, coming up behind her, chuckled softly. 'Don't tell me—Arnie Blackstone's giving you the pip.'

She turned and smiled at him. 'Isn't he just! Are you sure you couldn't discharge him yet?'

Tom laughed again. 'In the interests of my future career, I think we should perhaps keep him until he's on solids again, Sister Cooper!'

Helen rolled her eyes. 'Oh, if you insist. . .'

'Oh, but I do. I tell you what, to compensate, why don't I take you out for a drink tonight?'

Helen, desperately conscious not only of her own reaction but of Ruth and her insatiable curiosity just inches away, smiled brightly and panicked.

'Um—that would be lovely. Where shall we meet?'

'I'll pick you up—I have a rather special venue in mind. Say seven o'clock?'

'Fine. Right. I'll see you then.'

She turned away, and nearly fell over the drugs trolley, which brought a snort of laughter from Ruth and God knew what reaction from Tom. She was too busy hiding her confusion to dare to look at him.

'A date, eh?' Ruth murmured as he walked away, whistling softly. 'Now there's a turn-up for the books— or isn't it the first?'

Helen made a non-commital noise and busied herself

with the patient records on the computer. She would have to go over them all again because inevitably she was keying in absolute garbage, but she had to do something to stop herself from shrieking aloud with delight.

He had actually asked her out!

CHAPTER FOUR

TOM was a few minutes late, which was just as well, because it took Helen until after seven to make up her mind what to wear.

She had just pulled on the flowery leggings and long tunic top and was attempting to make something of her hair when the doorbell rang.

She slipped her feet into cotton shoes, grabbed her bag and a loose cotton pullover and then, drawing a deep breath to compose herself, she opened the door.

'Hi — all ready?'

She nodded. 'If I'm smart enough?'

He gave her a quick once-over and his mouth quirked in that familiar half-smile. 'You look fine. Come on, time's awasting.'

He opened the car door for her, closed it behind her and ran round the bonnet, whistling cheerfully. Something had obviously put him in a good mood, and she wasn't conceited enough to put it down to their date. Anyway, he had seemed happier all day.

'Where are we going?' she asked him.

He tapped the side of his nose. 'Secret. Just fasten your seatbelt and prepare to be amazed.'

She was more curious than ever, and as they headed out into the country her curiosity grew by leaps and bounds.

Then suddenly they were turning up the track that led to Rose Cottage, and pulling up on the drive. He jumped out and ran round, opening her door with a flourish.

She slid off the seat and stood up slowly, thoroughly bemused.

'Why are we at the Barringtons'?' she asked.

'Because,' he said with a smile, 'it's mine.'

'Yours?' she gasped. 'That quickly?'

'Yup! All signed and sealed—well, virtually. We don't actually complete the sale until next week, but we exchanged contracts late yesterday and Clare dropped the key in this morning. You're my first visitor.'

She followed him through the low doorway into the kitchen, and saw a new packet of wine glasses on the side.

'I hope you drink wine,' he said, and she nodded.

'Yes, of course. How exciting! I can't believe it's all happened so quickly!'

He grinned, looking like a child with a new toy. 'Great, isn't it? Here, let's open this and celebrate.' He took a bottle out of the fridge.

'Champagne!'

'Well—sort of.'

He pulled off the foil and slackened the wire, then popped the cork out of the back door. The wine foamed over the neck and dribbled on his hands, and he laughed and filled the glasses, then set the bottle down. 'Here.' He handed her a glass, and the bubbles tickled her nose, making her wrinkle it up.

'It tickles!' she said breathlessly.

His strange, fleeting smile came and went and he lifted the glass to her.

'Here's to the house,' he murmured.

She sipped the wine, then sipped again. 'Oh, it's

lovely. Cold and refreshing. Are you going to get me tiddly?'

He chuckled softly. 'Not intentionally. Come on, let's go and wander round.'

She followed him through into the other downstairs room. 'Gosh, it looks so empty!'

'Perhaps because it is?' he said drily.

'You know what I mean. I'm so used to Clare and Michael's clutter all over it, it seems really strange without.'

'I'll need some furniture — I haven't even got a bed yet, but I'm having one delivered tomorrow lunchtime. The trouble is I have to furnish it on a shoe-string, so I'll need to buy in the right places.'

'Auction sales?'

'Yes, and junk shops — know any good ones?'

She laughed in delight. 'Oh, yes — junk shops are my pet thing.'

His mouth tipped again. 'Give me a hand? I could use a little local knowledge.'

'Sure. Whenever you like.'

'Tomorrow?'

Her heart raced with the thought. 'Yes, tomorrow will be fine. It'll be fun.'

'Come and see upstairs — I've got a feeling this bed will dwarf the room, but I don't care, I can't stand little beds.'

'What have you bought, for heaven's sake? A seven-foot round one or something?'

He gave a surprised laugh. 'No, nothing so bizarre. Just a king-size double, but the rooms are tiny.'

'At least they left the carpets and curtains,' she commented as she followed him up.

'Yes, it's saved me a fortune — There, this is the room. Do you think a big bed will look too absurd?'

She looked round doubtfully. 'It isn't exactly a huge room, is it?'

He laughed shortly. 'No. Still, it's only me. I can always keep other things in the spare room, and I only need enough room to undress and get into it. I don't plan to do much entertaining up here.'

There was no easy way to follow that, so Helen took a large sip of her wine and made her way back downstairs.

'Can we look at the garden?' she asked him.

'Of course.'

He topped up her wine and then followed her out of the back door, and they strolled side by side round the beds, pausing every now and then to smell the flowers and look at interesting shrubs.

'It's very pretty, isn't it? Look, the clematis is flowering.'

Tom paused beside the arch, touching the delicate pink and white petals with a gentle finger, then moved on. 'So is the lilac — look, it's beautiful, and the scent is intoxicating.'

'You sure that's not the champagne?' she said with a laugh.

'Quite sure,' he murmured, and he broke off a tiny sprig of flowers and tucked it behind her ear. 'There. Now you look like a flower fairy.'

She blushed and giggled. 'You're nuts.'

'No.' He turned her towards him, and his eyes tracked slowly over her face. 'Ron Church was right, you know. You are lovely — very, very lovely.'

Her breath caught in her throat.

'Oh, Tom,' she whispered, just as his mouth came

down and brushed lightly over hers — once, twice —
then he lifted his head and turned away with a sigh.

'Tell me about yourself,' he said after a moment,
and his voice sounded strained and roughened.

It was a moment before she could speak, and then
she couldn't think of anything very riveting to say.

'There's not very much to tell — I'm twenty-seven. I
trained in Cambridge, I've been at the Audley four
years — that's about it, really.'

'That's not what I want to know,' he chided. 'What
are your likes and dislikes, what sort of music do you
listen to, whose books do you read — things like that.
Silly little things that make you what you are.'

'Oh. Well, I like all sorts of music — jazz, blues,
classical, some pop — all sorts. And I read thrillers
and romances and books about the Third Reich and
regency novels — the only things I really hate are
psychological thrillers and violence.'

His smile flashed white in the gathering gloom.
'Eclectic taste,' he said softly.

'My brother says I just can't make up my mind, but
I think that's so narrow. Why should I dismiss so much
just because one area has particular appeal? And
anyway I like change.'

'Me too,' he agreed.

'Your turn,' she told him.

'Me?' He sounded surprised. 'I'm very boring. I like
mainly classical music, some blues. I hate country
music, can't stand barn dances and like historical
novels — Ken Follett for instance — and science fiction.
That's when I have time, which at the moment I don't.'

They turned back towards the house. 'How's the
studying going?' she asked.

'Oh, not so bad. I worked last night late, but I'm still

not getting in enough time. Perhaps once I'm sleeping here rather than the hospital residence things will be better.'

'When's the viva?'

He groaned. 'Thursday.'

'Oh, dear. Well, we'll have to get your furniture sorted out as quickly as we can.'

'Starting tomorrow. What time shall I pick you up?'

'Whenever you like — nine?'

'Done. We'd better lock up the cottage and I'll take you home — I have to get in some studying tonight or I can't spent tomorrow gallivanting round the countryside hunting old bits of junk!'

He gave her the champagne bottle to carry, and, once in his car, they wound their way back through the country lanes, the may blossom gleaming brightly in the gloom of the evening.

'I think May is probably my favourite month,' Helen said with a sigh. 'Everything bursting into life, all the birds singing — wonderful. Sort of renewing, somehow.'

He shot her a teasing glance. 'You old romantic, you.'

'Oh, I am. I believe in all sorts of crazy things, like love at first sight — I even believe in marriage. My brother says I'm stupid, that marriage is a shackle and a waste of time, but I don't agree. I think if you make the commitment of marriage vows, then you're more likely to stay together — especially if you take the vows to heart. So many people don't these days.'

Tom was silent, and Helen could feel him withdrawing. Oh, lord, had she put her foot in it again? Was he married? Was that it? Had his wife left him? If so, it must be for good, because he kept saying he would be on his own in the cottage.

'You obviously don't agree,' she said softly, to draw him out.

He pulled up outside her flat and stared straight ahead, unblinking. 'On the contrary,' he said expressionlessly. 'I think you're absolutely right.' He took a deep breath and let it out on a sigh, then, with an obvious effort to shake off his mood, he turned towards her and smiled. 'So, I'll see you in the morning at nine.'

She searched his face. The smile didn't reach his eyes, not by a long way. 'Fine. I'll be ready. Thanks for the drink — here.' She passed him the half-finished bottle of champagne.

'Don't you want it?' he asked.

'No — I've had enough. It might help you study.'

He gave a dry laugh. 'Some chance. Never mind. I'll see you tomorrow.'

He stayed in the car, watching till she was through the door before driving off into the night.

She watched his tail-lights through the window, and then made herself a drink and settled down to watch the television. It was still fairly early — far too early to go to bed and hope to sleep.

Perhaps the television would take her mind off the enigma that was Tom Russell, but it was unlikely. It would have to be far more riveting than usual to stand the slightest chance.

'How about this?'

'It's a picture, Tom. You can't sit on it.'

'I like it.'

'It's fifty pounds. Put it down and come on!'

He set the picture down with a sigh and followed her out of the shop.

'Where to now?'

'A place that specialises in old pine.'

'You don't think I want oak?'

'Not unless you can afford sixteenth-century oak.'

'Hmm. I tell you what—why don't you find me the things and I'll just write out the cheques?'

She laughed. 'You're very trusting.'

'No, I just know when I'm licked.'

Their laughter mingled in the warm air, and as they wound their way through the little streets around the old part of the town Helen began to wonder if she hadn't imagined his reluctance. Perhaps he was just shy and liked to take things slowly? Whatever, he was certainly throwing himself into today with a vengeance.

They found the pine shop, and within a few minutes she had chosen a couple of chests of drawers, a bed for his spare room and a table and chairs for the kitchen, all well within his budget. He paid and arranged for delivery, and then Helen led him out of the shop.

'Now for the sitting-room,' she said briskly, and Tom obediently followed her directions, pulling up outside another junk shop.

'That looks nice,' Tom said, eyeing a three-piece suite.

'Too big for your cottage. Here, this is better and it will go with the curtains.'

He conceded laughingly, and they also picked up a bedside table, a couple of bedroom chairs and an occasional table for the sitting-room.

'What about kitchen things—crockery, cutlery, pans and stuff like that?'

'I need everything except a kettle.'

She took him to another shop, a kitchen reject shop where he bought everything except the kitchen sink, and they staggered back to the car laden down with their purchases.

'Right, how much money have you got left from your budget? she asked him.

He grinned. 'Just enough for the picture.'

'Oh, Tom!'

'Well, I need pictures on the wall. Let's go and haggle.'

They beat the man down to thirty-five pounds, how Helen had no idea, and then drove back to the cottage.

There was a hook between the windows on a blank stretch of wall, and Tom hung the picture on it and stood back.

'You were right,' she told him. 'It looks good there. It's very evocative.'

It was a watercolour of a path leading through trees, and in the distance the sky gleamed, like the light at the end of a long dark tunnel.

'It's called *Hope*,' she told him, squinting at the writing in the bottom corner.

'I know.'

His voice was strange, flat and yet somehow expressive, and Helen turned.

He was looking at her, his eyes burning strangely, and she felt her heart beat faster. Then he looked away, his movements jerky and strained, and walked off into the kitchen.

'Cup of tea?'

She followed him hesitantly and leant against the wall, arms wrapped round her waist defensively. 'Thanks, that would be lovely.'

She watched him as he filled the kettle and plugged it in, then stood looking out of the window at the garden, his back to her.

'Thanks for all your help,' he said eventually, and his voice sounded normal again, more resonant. She heaved a quiet sigh of relief.

'My pleasure. I told you, I love junk shops.'

He turned back towards her, his smile fleeting. 'Yes, of course. It shows. I could do with some more pictures and bits and pieces — are you busy this afternoon?'

She shook her head. 'No, not at all, but I thought you'd run out of money.'

His mouth twitched. 'Well, not exactly. I've got almost everything on an unrealistic budget, so I reckon I can treat myself a little now. How about a cheese sandwich for lunch while we wait for this bed to be delivered?'

'Sure.'

She helped him make them, and they ate them in the garden under the apple trees, with the heady scent of the lilac and the steady drone of bees for company. There was no trace of whatever had touched him earlier, no lingering darkness in his eyes, and she began to wonder if she had imagined it again.

The bed was delivered shortly after they had finished, and Tom and the delivery man struggled with it up the steep, narrow stairs and over the banisters under the eaves.

'There,' Tom said with satisfaction as he fixed the headboard and stood back. 'It doesn't look too bad, does it?'

It looked, Helen thought, unbelievably tempting. She turned his attention fast to practical matters.

'Have you got sheets and things?'

'No, we can get them now. Are you ready to go?'

'When you are.'

He shot her a fleeting grin. 'So let's go.'

The afternoon was wonderful and after they had bought the linen they had great fun together fossicking about among the boxes of oddments outside all the junk shops.

They found a few plates to put on the wall over the inglenook, a couple of lamps and pictures for the sitting-room, and a whole collection of music, which delighted Tom.

'Why do you want music?' she asked him as they unloaded it all.

'For the piano.'

She laughed. 'But you haven't got a piano!'

He smiled slightly. 'I have. It's in storage; I'll get it next week. Do you play?'

'No.' She wrinkled her nose in disgust. 'I had lessons at school but I was useless.'

'You ought to try again.'

She smiled slightly. 'I don't think so, not in my flat. It's too embarrassing.'

'You'll have to practise here. I'll go and dig the garden or something so I'm not putting you off.'

'We'll see. Once you've heard me you probably won't let me near it in case I damage it!'

He chuckled. 'Helen, you're crazy.'

They were standing in the sitting-room, just a couple of feet apart, and suddenly the atmosphere between them was charged with tension.

She hardly dared to breathe in case she did the wrong thing, but then his eyes flicked away from her to the painting on the wall, and he sighed softly.

'I'd better take you home; I've taken up enough of your weekend.'

She didn't argue. The mood was lost, and anyway, she was finding his company very demanding. Every time she thought they were getting somewhere, he withdrew into his shell again and left her standing on the outside, confused. Even so, she wanted to be with him, but it was emotionally draining. She would have given her eye-teeth for a day alone with him — without whatever it was that hovered like a threat between them, destroying every intimate moment.

The next week was hectic in the extreme. Ross covered as much as he could for Tom to give him time to study for his viva, and they were both fairly tired and short-tempered as a result.

Helen kept out of their way, and made sure the new coffee-jug was kept permanently full. Even Tom was piling through it at a rate of knots, and as the day of his exam drew nearer Helen grew more an more concerned for him.

He was tight-lipped and silent, and on the day before he was due to go down to London she collared him on the ward and dragged him into the office.

'What are you doing tonight?'

He stared at her as if she were mad.

'Revising.'

'Rubbish. You've done enough. Come for supper.'

'Helen, I can't —'

'Of course you can. You have to eat — I'm not asking you to stay late, but what you don't know now you never will, and you look shattered.'

He sighed, then gave a short, humourless laugh. 'I am shattered.'

'So come.'

He nodded in resignation. 'OK. Thanks. What time?'

'Whenever you're ready. Do you fancy chicken?'

'Oh, don't go to a lot of trouble, Helen. I'm really not very hungry at the moment.'

She eyed him critically. 'No, I can see you've lost weight. Just come, Tom, and eat as much or as little as you want. You've been on your own too much recently.'

His eyes burned into her face, and with a short laugh he turned away. 'Don't lecture me, Helen. I really don't need it.'

He walked out of the room and left her staring after him, wondering why she was bothering with him.

Mrs Tranter was going home that afternoon, and would be starting her radiotherapy and chemotherapy in the next couple of weeks. There was no likelihood of being able to stop the spread of the cancer, but the treatment should control its progress to a degree and certainly keep her considerably more pain-free than she would otherwise be. And, as she said herself, she was better off than Ron Church.

Helen detailed Carol, the second-year student, to help Mrs Tranter dress and pack all her things, and then together they stripped down the bed and prepared it for the next patient.

Although they were busy most of the cases were fairly routine and followed a predictable course, which provided an ideal learning situation for Carol, and Helen had been able to show her the less dramatic side of ward life following her somewhat shaky start with Ron Church's death and Judy Fulcher's husband's violent behaviour.

Judy was making only slow progress, and Ross was resigned to taking her back to Theatre to drain an abscess in the left side of her abdomen that had formed as a result of the rupture of her appendix.

Her slow progress suited Judy, though. She was in no hurry to be discharged, especially since her husband was at home waiting to punish her for his humiliating eviction from the hospital.

Security had been tightened up, and there had been no further incidents, but still she was uneasy and Helen was very worried about what lay in store for her once she left.

Amazingly nothing unpredictable happened that afternoon, and Helen was able to get away promptly. She called in at a local supermarket on her way and picked up some chicken pieces and vegetables, and went home to throw together a chicken marengo.

At six, when her hair was wet from the shower and she was dressed only in a pair of jeans and a T-shirt, the doorbell rang.

'You're early,' she accused him laughingly, standing in the hallway in bare feet.

'You said come when I was ready—do you want me to go away again for a bit?'

'No, of course not. Come in.' She took his arm and towed him through into the kitchen. 'Here—have a drink, and sit and talk to me while I do these beans.'

He lifted the lid of the casserole and sniffed. 'Gosh, that smells good.'

She smiled. 'Hungry?'

His expression was wry. 'Yes—very. Bless you, Helen.'

She turned away, confused by the tenderness in his eyes. 'You're welcome. Pour me a glass of wine, will you?'

He set it down beside her, and he leaned against the worktop and watched as she topped and tailed the fine green beans. She tried not to let it put her off, but even so she nearly cut herself a couple of times.

'God, it smells fantastic,' he said as she dished up a little while later.

She eyed him over the top of the casserole. 'When did you last eat?'

'Properly?' He shrugged. 'I don't remember.'

'Oh, Tom. . .' She ladled the rich, tasty sauce over the tender chicken and handed him the plate. 'Here, help yourself to veg.'

He did — and ate every last scrap, coming back twice for more.

Afterwards he slouched on her sofa with a cup of coffee and regarded her sleepily. 'Helen, that was. . .' Lost for words, he put his fingertips together and kissed them. 'Fantastic. Marvellous. I feel human again.'

'Good.' She was touched by his praise, and self-consciously delighted. 'Now what you have to do is get a good night's sleep and stop worrying.'

He snorted. 'Fat chance. What if I fail?'

'You won't fail.'

'I might already have failed the written papers.'

'So why worry about tomorrow?'

He laughed softly. 'Why, indeed? OK, I'll take your advice and go home to bed, and then tomorrow I'll knock their socks off.'

She walked him to the door, and after a second's hesitation he bent his head and kissed her lightly on the lips. 'Thanks, Helen. You're wonderful.'

She opened the door and watched him go. 'Break a leg,' she called after him, and he waved and grinned.

The next day seemed endless. She kept a close eye on her watch, and thought of Tom constantly. First he would have his viva, then the clinical examination, and then at the end of the day the names of those who had passed would be read out and they would have a drink and sign the big red book, giving their commitment to the Royal College of Surgeons and vowing to uphold their good name — if he got that far. If not, he would come home, doubtless with his ego severely battered and his professional tail between his legs.

Ross operated on Judy, and using a laparoscope found a big pocket of pus under her bowel which was threatening to turn into a very nasty abscess. He drained it using a needle, and he was hopeful that she would now start to make more rapid progress.

'I wonder how Tom's doing?' Ross said when he came down later that afternoon to look at his post-ops.'

'Goodness knows. I can't think about anything else.'

Ross eyed her thoughtfully. 'He means a lot to you, doesn't he?'

She met his eyes and then looked away, unable to handle it. Ross saw too much in people's eyes. That was why he was such a good doctor, and such a perceptive and thoughtful colleague. It also made him very difficult to keep secrets from.

'Sometimes I think maybe he could come to mean a lot — at other times, he's just another colleague.'

Ross snorted softly. 'If you say so, Helen. Right, I must get on. If you see Gavin, send him down to the clinic, could you?'

'Sure.'

She was kept too busy for the rest of the day to think very much, but that evening she sat by the phone, with no real hope that he would call her, willing it to ring.

At midnight she went to bed, and in the morning she made her way to work tired and depressed.

He could have rung, she thought crossly, and then chided herself. Why should he, after all? What was she to him but a colleague? Nothing, probably. Maybe they had the beginnings of a new friendship, but certainly there was nothing else between them, no reason why he should have called her.

She was still telling herself off when she went into her office, and found Ross in there with Tom, looking absolutely deadpan.

'Well?' she asked finally, her heart in her mouth.

Not even Tom could keep the smile from his face.

'You passed?' she said excitedly.

'I passed.'

'Tom, that's fantastic!' she cried, and threw her arms round him, hugging him hard. 'Oh, that is the most wonderful news!'

He hugged her back and then released her, looking down at her with a rueful grin. 'I meant to ring you last night to let you know, but I ran into some old friends and we ended up celebrating somewhat. I drove up this morning, and I must say I feel a bit ragged!'

'Ragged but victorious, eh? I tell you what——' Ross fished in his jacket pocket '—use these and go and celebrate. Lizzi and I were going, but we're just too tired and Lizzi isn't up to it at the moment, so you two go.'

He handed Tom a pair of tickets.

'What is it?' Helen asked.

'The RMBF May Ball, on Saturday. Can you use them?'

Tom hesitated.

'Perhaps he would rather take someone else?' Helen said quietly.

'No,' he murmured. 'I'd like to take you, if you'd like to go?'

'I'd love to, Tom. Thank you.'

'Great.' Ross grinned. 'Right, back to the grind. You've got a clinic, *Mr* Russell, and I've got patients to see.'

The last ball Helen had been to was a Hunt Ball at home one Christmas some five and a half years before and she literally had nothing suitable to wear.

It was a good excuse to indulge herself, and she did, without a qualm.

It was only when she had piled her hair on top of her head and was putting the finishing touches to her make-up that she had a twinge of panic.

The dress was blue, a wonderful deep lavender-blue, made of silk taffeta, with a strapless fitted bodice and a full ballerina-length skirt that set off her tiny waist and showed a peep of calf above her ankles.

She had found some tights with a tiny sparkle in, and even bought some spray glitter for her hair.

When she looked in the mirror, she saw the glitter had drifted and settled on her skin, giving the pale gold a delicate sheen and emphasising the fine bones of her shoulders. She looked beautiful, she realised with astonishment — like a woman poised on the brink of discovery.

The doorbell rang, and she moistened her lips, suddenly nervous.

'Don't be silly, it's only Tom,' she told herself, out loud and, wrapping a stole round her shoulders, she went to the door.

He looked incredible, the shirt gleaming white against his skin, the immaculate fit of his dinner-jacket setting off his broad shoulders and slim waist to perfection.

In his hands he held an orchid. 'I thought you might like to wear this,' he said, and his voice was husky.

'Oh — thank you,' she breathed. No one had ever brought her a corsage before, and she was inexplicably touched. 'Where — where shall I —— ?'

'How about your hair?'

He took it from her trembling fingers and tucked in into the side of her hair over her ear, then stood back and looked at her.

She twirled slowly. 'Will I do?'

He looked faintly thunderstruck. 'Oh, yes, I think so.' His mouth quirked slightly, and the appreciation in his eyes was plain to see. 'Are you ready?'

She nodded. 'Yes — yes, I'm ready.'

They arrived at the country club and were quickly swept into the glittering throng, but they could have been quite alone.

At first, when they danced, he held her slightly away from him, but by the end of the evening her head was on his shoulder and his hands lay clasped behind her back, drawing her against him as they swayed together to the music.

They might have danced together for years, Helen thought dreamily as she moved slowly in time to the music. Her head fitted just right against his shoulder, and as she breathed she caught the fragrance of his cologne, lemon with a touch of musk, a heady combination. He eased her closer so that their feet were meshed together and his thighs were firm against hers, shifting as he swayed.

She wanted to stay there forever in his arms, cradled against his chest, oblivious to the world.

Finally the MC climbed on to the stage with the band and Tom released her reluctantly while the man thanked everyone for their presence and announced the last waltz. Then she melted into his arms one last time.

As the strains of the music died away and everyone applauded, Tom led her off the dance-floor.

'Come on, let's see if we can get out before the crush,' he murmured, and she collected her stole and bag and they made their way to the car.

They drove back to her flat in silence, and all the way Helen wondered what would happen. Should she invite him in? Offer him coffee? Or just thank him and say goodbye?

Would he even want to come in?

By the time he drew up outside the flat, she was no nearer a conclusion.

He took the decision out of her hands. 'Are you going to offer me a coffee?' he suggested.

'Would you like one?'

'I don't know. I just know I don't want this evening to end,' he said honestly.

She reached out and took his hand, encouraged by his honesty. 'Neither do I. It's been a lovely evening, Tom. I've had a wonderful time.'

'Me, too.' He lifted her hand to his lips and kissed it gently. 'Come on, then. Let's go inside.'

She flicked on the lights in the sitting-room, and then lit a couple of candles before turning off the overhead light.

'More atmospheric,' she said with a laugh.

He was eyeing her strangely, his expression unreadable in the flickering glow. She made the coffee and brought it in, then perched on the chair opposite.

He patted the sofa beside him. 'Come and sit down,' he said softly.

She moved, settling herself in the corner, her feet tucked up under her bottom, and gave her coffee more attention than it really merited.

He was watching her, she could tell, and she found it faintly unnerving. 'So — tell me about Thursday,' she said at last.

'Oh — well, it was hell! I was sure I got everything wrong. The clinical was tricky, too —— Helen, that dress is really beautiful on you.'

She flicked him a startled glance. 'Dress?'

He reached out a hand and touched the silk. 'It feels incredible. Did you buy it specially?

'Yes — it was a dreadful extravagance, but I loved it on sight.'

'It was worth every penny, believe me,' he said huskily. His hand ran up her arm, his fingers warm and firm against her skin. 'You're all shimmering — it's fascinating. Lord, your skin is so soft. . .'

His fingertips trailed lightly over her throat, then down to run slowly around the top of the bodice. Her breath caught in her throat and she turned to look at him, surprising a look of naked desire that set her ablaze.

'Oh, Tom,' she whispered, and then she was in his arms, his body stretched out against hers, and he was kissing her as though he were dying and only she could save him.

His hands found the zip in the side of her dress, and in the next instant her breasts were free and his mouth was suckling greedily at them, first one, then the other.

She plunged her hands into his hair and cradled his

head against her, aching for him with a need that was
beyond reason.

'Oh, Tom, make love to me, please,' she begged,
and as she said the words he lifted his head, his eyes
wide and shocked, and dragged himself away.

'No, Helen,' he groaned, his voice raw with pain.

'Why, Tom?' she asked unsteadily. 'We're both
free—why shouldn't we?' A cold feeling of dread was
curling round her heart, and as she watched him he
turned towards her and she saw despair in his eyes.

'But that's just it,' he said raggedly. 'I'm not free,
Helen. I'm married—and there's not a damn thing I
can do about it!'

CHAPTER FIVE

FOR a second, Helen was frozen, immobilised with shock. Then her movement returned, on a great wave of anger, and she raised her arm and slapped his face with all the force she could muster.

'Bastard!' she hissed, and, dragging up the bodice of her gown, she ran past him into the bedroom and yanked off the dress, throwing it into the corner. The orchid was next, its petals crushed and broken, and then the tights.

She tugged open a drawer and pulled out a T-shirt, dragging it on over her head, then looked for her jeans.

He had followed her and was standing in the doorway watching her, his face unreadable. 'What are you doing?'

'I'm changing,' she said shortly, shoving her legs ruthlessly into her jeans. 'What the hell does it look like? I'm going for a walk.'

'Not at this time of night: it isn't safe ——'

'Safe?' She laughed hysterically. 'What would you call being here with you? Damn you, Tom, how could you?'

'You don't understand ——'

'Oh, that's what they all say. I suppose your wife doesn't understand you either! Where is she, Tom?' she raved. 'What does she think you're doing here in Suffolk all on your own — twiddling your thumbs?'

His face was like granite, and his voice was deathly quiet. 'She doesn't think anything. She's in a clinic near

84

Norwich. She was brain damaged in an avalanche three years ago, and she's in PVS—persistent vegetative state. She doesn't even know who I am.'

Helen felt all the fight drain out of her, leaving behind it a sickening emptiness. 'Oh, dear God—oh, Tom. I'm so sorry. . .'

His eyes held hers, their expression tortured. 'I'm sorry I involved you. I never meant this to happen, but when Ross offered us the tickets I thought it would give me a legitimate reason to hold you in my arms. I never thought——'

He broke off, his breathing unsteady, and suddenly Helen couldn't bear it any more. For three weeks now she had watched him suffer and not known why. Now, the least she could do was comfort him.

She wrapped her arms round him and held him close, and after a moment his arms slid over hers and he clung to her, his face buried in her hair.

'Oh, Helen, help me,' he pleaded. 'I need you so much. Don't shut me out, for God's sake.'

'I won't shut you out, Tom,' she murmured. 'Come on—come and sit down and tell me all about it.'

He followed her through to the sitting-room, and then he pulled her on to his lap and held her close while he told her the story in a heart-rending monotone that did nothing to conceal his suffering.

They had gone skiing, he said. It was March and rather late in the season, and the snow was a bit unstable, but Juliette was an experienced skier and so he thought it would be all right.

'There was an avalanche—nothing very big, but she was caught by it. It was several minutes before I found her, and then more still before I managed to free her from the snow. I thought she was dead for sure, but then she started breathing again.'

He gave a short laugh. 'I couldn't believe it. She was going to be all right, I thought. Then the ambulance came and took her to hospital in Innsbruck, and they told me she was in coma. Gradually over the next couple of days her level of consciousness rose, but only to the extent of reflex. She has no upper cerebral function, no recognition, nothing of herself left. Sometimes she's awake, sometimes she's asleep. Always she's totally unresponsive. She can't communicate her needs, she's tube-fed, catheterised and incontinent. And yet she's still my wife.'

That statement, quietly delivered, gave Helen more clues to Tom than anything else she had heard. 'Is there any hope?' she asked, knowing as she did that there could be none.

He shook his head. 'No. No, there's no hope. She's as she is, and that's it. I go and visit her every Sunday, and during the week if I can, and I talk to her and tell her what's been going on, but I know she can't understand me. It helps to pass the time, though.'

'Oh, Tom,' Helen said heavily. 'I am so, so sorry.'

'I can't leave her, Helen. You do realise that, don't you? I'll never leave her, and I'll never be unfaithful to her. I married her for better or for worse, and this is a lot worse than I ever imagined, but I know she'd do the same for me. I'm just sorry you got involved.'

She smoothed his hair back from his brow and traced the line of his cut, now healed. 'I knew all along there was something wrong — all those times I thought you were going to kiss me, and then you didn't — I thought I'd done something to upset you.'

He hugged her gently. 'No — no, you did nothing to

upset me. My equilibrium, yes, but not me. Believe me, I wanted to kiss you — desperately.'

'Why didn't you tell me?'

He shrugged. 'I didn't want sympathy — in a way I just wanted — oh, I don't know. It wasn't really deliberate, and I've been trying to find a way to tell you for several days now, but — I just didn't seem to be able to find the words. Anyway ——' he shrugged '— I thought I'd be able to keep it platonic, to have fun with you and just keep it on a friendly footing.'

He gave a short, humourless laugh. 'What a bloody fool I was. I should have realised what you were coming to mean to me, but I suppose I just didn't let myself see it. I think I needed you too much to risk losing you.'

His eyes met hers, and the longing in them made her want to weep. The imprint of her hand was clearly visible on his cheek, and she laid her palm against it as if to take away the pain.

'Tom, what are we going to do?'

'Nothing,' he said flatly. 'There's nothing we can do. We're trapped, Helen — trapped, and there's no way out.'

He stood up and set her gently on her feet. 'I'd better go home now, before it's too late.' He bent and brushed her lips with his, and then moments later he was gone.

Too late? It was already too late, she thought miserably.

She took the coffee-cups through to the kitchen, set them in the sink and then went into her bedroom. The ballgown was lying crumpled in the corner, and she picked it up and smoothed the skirt out, then hung it up in the back of her wardrobe where she wouldn't have to look at it.

But she couldn't put away the image of Tom's eyes, stark with despair and loneliness, and yet resolute. He would be, of course. He was like that.

A man of honour.

'Oh, Tom,' she whispered brokenly, and, curling up on the bed, she buried her face in the pillow and wept.

Sunday was long—longer than any other day had ever been. She wanted to talk to Tom, to tell him it was all right, that she understood, but he wasn't at home.

Visiting Juliette in Norwich, of course, she realised belatedly after she had tried to ring him several times. He had said he always went on Sundays.

But she knew she couldn't just go to work on Monday morning without having seen him again and sorted out the parameters of their relationship— because, like it or not, they did have a relationship. Doomed to failure, of course, but there nevertheless, and perhaps they could salvage something from the tangled wreckage that would help them both to deal with their lives.

If he even wanted to know.

He still wasn't back by ten on Sunday night, so she got up early on Monday morning and drove out to the cottage, arriving shortly after six.

'You're probably the last person he wants to see,' she told herself aloud as she turned and bumped up the drive, but she steeled herself, took a deep breath and rang the doorbell.

He answered it moments later, clad only in a towelling robe, his hair dripping on to the collar. His eyes flickered with something unreadable, then were carefully blanked. 'Come in,' he said evenly. 'I was in the shower—give me a minute and I'll be down.'

She watched him go, then filled the kettle and switched it on. Perhaps she could do this better over a cup of tea.

She could hear him moving around in the room above, opening and shutting drawers, and then he was running lightly down the stairs, to come to a halt just feet away from her.

'What brings you here?' he asked, his voice expressionless.

She didn't know how to start. 'I—I just felt—I couldn't go in to work without talking to you, and you weren't here yesterday——'

'I was with Juliette,' he told her, his voice unyielding. It was as if he felt he had to bring her name up, to bring her into the room with them so that neither of them forgot what this was all about.

As if they would.

'I know where you were,' Helen replied quietly. 'I just wanted to apologise for going off the deep end on Saturday night. I was pretty upset.'

'Yes, well, I'm sorry about that. You were right, I should have told you. I should never have let things go so far——'

'Far? Come on, Tom, things went nowhere. You've never encouraged me, or given me any reason to believe that we were ever going to have a relationship.'

He met her eyes, his own frank at last. 'Haven't I? What about the weekend we went shopping for my furniture? Is that something you do with someone you're trying to discourage?'

'That depends what you're trying to discourage them from. It was really a very platonic day—I could just as easily have been a man, Tom. A friend.'

'I kissed you in the garden,' he said, his voice raw.

His eyes were filled with longing, and she looked away, her resolve weakening. 'Only briefly.'

'It wasn't brief the other night, and I didn't want to stop——'

'But you did stop! That's the point. Just because you want to make love to me it doesn't mean you have to!'

She moved over to him, unable to say what she had to say without his strength.

Taking his hands in hers, she looked up into his tortured face. 'You asked me not to shut you out, Tom. You asked for my help, and that's why I'm here—to offer it. We can't deny that we're attracted to each other, but we can be honest, and we can control our actions and the direction of our relationship. I just wanted you to know that if you need me—as a friend— I'm here for you. Now I have to go——'

She turned away, her eyes blurred with tears, but he pulled her back against his chest and wrapped his arms round her.

'Thank you,' he whispered. 'You don't know how much that means——' His voice cracked, and his arms tightened round her in a wordless hug of comfort.

After a moment she eased away, afraid that if she stayed there her resolve would disintegrate.

'How about a cup of tea?' she suggested, and her voice was strangled.

His was little better. 'The universal British panacea.' He laughed shortly, then sighed. 'It's probably not a bad idea. Have you had breakfast?'

And so they proceeded to have tea and toast, just as if nothing had happened—but it had. In the space of a few weeks Helen had fallen in love, and nothing would ever be the same again.

* * *

Ross came down after his list and wandered, whistling, into her office. She was standing at the window staring out, and heard him reach for the coffee-pot.

'Morning! How was the ball?'

'Lovely,' she said, but her voice was mechanical.

She heard him come up behind her, and then his hands on her shoulders turned her to face him.

'Helen?' His voice was soft, concerned, and suddenly it was all too much.

Her eyes blurred, and the next thing she knew she was wrapped hard against his chest and was pouring it all out, her feelings for Tom, the shock of finding out he was married, and the worse shock of dicovering that Juliette was hovering in the shadows of life, not dead and yet not alive.

'Oh, Helen — God, I'm so sorry,' Ross murmured into her hair. 'I knew he'd been married, but I thought he was divorced now. If I'd had any idea I wouldn't have pushed you together —— '

'You didn't, Ross. There's been something there between us since the first time we met.'

He nodded and let her go, pressing a tissue into her hand. 'I thought as much. Here, dry your eyes before someone comes in and gets curious.'

He poured her a cup of coffee and pushed her into a chair, then perched on the other one, leaning towards her, his eyes concerned.

'Where do you go from here?'

She shrugged helplessly. 'There's nowhere to go, Ross. He's married, he won't leave her, and I couldn't possibly ask him to. He takes his vows very seriously, and so do I. I wouldn't dream of having an affair with a married man, and Juliette being in a persistent vegetative state just makes it worse. I mean, it's such an unfair fight. What weapons has she got?'

Ross stood up and refilled his cup. 'Clearly she's got a very powerful weapon—Tom's loyalty. I think you're right—he's not the sort of person to abandon her, even if there's nothing he can do to help her. He's trapped by himself, by his own sense of honour, and that's the hardest thing to overcome.'

Helen shook her head. 'It makes it easier, in a way. I can respect him for that, and I do. I'd find it much harder to love him if he weren't taking that stand. Is that crazy?'

Ross smiled, a crooked, gentle smile. 'No,' he said softly. 'No, Helen, it's not crazy. He's lucky to have met you, you know. You've got a deep sense of rightness that'll help you both to survive this, but it'll be very hard. You do realise, I suppose, that she could last for years?'

She nodded numbly. 'Yes, I know.'

'You'll have times when you'll want her to die, and that's very destructive emotionally. You might be better to cut your losses and forget him.'

She turned wide, shocked eyes to his. 'I couldn't do that, Ross! He needs me!'

Ross's smile was understanding. 'Now, how did I know you'd say that? Drink your coffee.'

'I've had stacks of coffee. What I need is an anaesthetic.'

'So why don't you go home for the rest of the day?'

'And run away? That won't help, Ross.'

He sighed. 'No, I suppose you're right. I must get on, I've got a clinic to do. If you see Tom, could you ask him to come down? Oh, and tell Gavin to keep an eye on Judy. She may be getting another abscess.'

Helen nodded. 'OK.'

Ross gave her a consoling wink and left for his clinic, and after a couple of seconds Helen stood up, washed the cups in the sink and headed for the ward. Perhaps some hard work would help to take her mind off Tom. Somehow she doubted it.

For the next few days their meetings were brief and rather strained, and as if by some unwritten rule they kept all conversation to professional exchanges.

It wasn't enough. Helen felt an overwhelming need to talk to Tom, to ask him about Juliette, as if by understanding more about her she could discover what it was that held him.

Was it simply his sense of honour, or had she earned his devotion? How long had they been married? Were they happy? What did she look like?

By the weekend she was unable to put her questions off any longer. On Saturday morning she got up, showered and dressed in jeans and a T-shirt and made her way to the cottage.

She found him in the garden, digging.

He looked up and smiled guardedly. 'Hi.'

'Hi.'

He frowned and peered at her more closely. 'What's wrong?'

She shrugged, unsure how to start. 'I just wanted to talk to you. Perhaps it wasn't such a good idea ——'

She turned and walked away, and after a few seconds she heard his long stride catching up with her.

'Stop! Helen, wait.'

'Oh, it's no good,' she said unsteadily. 'I thought I could be sensible, but I can't. I just want to be with you, to talk to you, to spend time together ——'

He pulled her into his arms, one hand cradling the

back of her head and holding it against his shoulder, the other stroking soothingly up and down her spine. 'I want to be with you, too. You're all I can think about, day and night. What the hell are we going to do?'

She sniffed hard and pushed away from him, wrapping her arms around her waist as if she could comfort herself by doing so. 'Nothing. As you said yourself, there's nothing we can do.'

'But we can't ignore it. Maybe if we face it, talk about it — perhaps it won't be quite so bad.'

She walked across the garden to the bench tucked it under the lilac, and sat down, hands clamped between her knees.

'Tell me about Juliette.'

'Juliette?' He sat beside her, his long legs stretched out, and sighed. 'What do you want to know?'

'Everything — what she looks like, how you felt about her, how long you'd been married, what her favourite colour was — anything — everything. Anything that might help me understand how you're feeling.'

He let out his breath slowly. 'OK. Well, she's a little taller than you, not as thin — well, she never used to be. She's painfully thin now, of course — her muscles have wasted, and she weighs practically nothing. But before — she was full of fun, always laughing, often at herself. She had a wicked sense of humour, but she never used it unkindly. Her hair's a sort of dark red — chestnut, I suppose — and long. They wanted to cut it in the clinic, but I wouldn't let them. They said it would be too hard to look after, but she loved her hair. It was her crowning glory, so every Sunday morning I wash it for her and blow-dry it.' He sighed. 'I know it's stupid, but she's lost so much, and it was just one last thing I could stop them taking away from her.'

He sighed again, deep in thought, then breathed in and straightened. 'Her favourite colour was rich fuchsia-pink, which was ridiculous with her hair but she got away with it somehow. That was how I found her — her salopettes were bright pink.'

He went quiet for a minute, and Helen sat there, motionless, afraid to disturb his thoughts. After a while he started speaking again.

'We met in our house year. We were both at the Radcliffe in Oxford, and we fell in love and got married without telling anyone somewhere in the middle of a hundred-and-twenty-hour weeks and no sleep, with hardly time to speak between shifts. It was amazing we survived it, but we did. Her parents said we wouldn't, and I think there was probably an element of bloody-mindedness that kept us going, but somehow we got through intact.

'Then we were separated. I stayed at the Radcliffe, Juliette was at the Royal Berks in Reading. Astonishingly we saw more of each other as registrars in different hospitals than we had as house doctors in the same one. She wanted to specialise in Obs and Gynae — she loved babies. She wanted to go and work in a Third World country when she'd got her MRCOG, but her parents were dead against it. They thought it was my influence, but it wasn't. It was her idea.'

He laughed softly, and his smile was full of tenderness. 'She was given to sweeping romantic gestures, but that was different. She really wanted to go somewhere — Africa, India — and use her talent to alleviate some of the appalling suffering.'

'Would you have gone too?'

He laughed again. 'Oh, yes. She had a way of convincing people that they wanted to do things that would never have occurred to them. She could have persuaded me to go anywhere and do anything— mainly to keep her out of mischief! She had no fear. We went to Marrakech once, and it was a miracle I got her out alive. She was too inquisitive for her own good. I think she also imagined she was immortal.'

He fell silent, staring at his hands, and Helen felt a terrible, gentle sadness steal over her.

'She sounds wonderful.'

'She was.' His voice was gruff, and he stood up and walked away, his shoulders bowed, and carried on with digging.

Helen wanted to cry for him. He had lost so much, and yet he wasn't free to forget or to start again.

There was no way she could compete with Juliette, with her wit and looks and charm that he had conjured so evocatively for her. He had obviously loved her very deeply—possibly he still did. Certainly her memory was still very vivid in his mind.

Perhaps, though, in Helen he might find a sort of solace, a companionship to fill the hours and days of his lonely vigil. She knew she could never take Juliette's place in his heart, and she wouldn't want to try, but if she could simply ease his pain that would be reward enough.

All she needed was the strength to give him her love, and ask nothing in return.

'Oh, God, help me be strong,' she whispered. 'Help me to help him. Help me to love him. Help me not to hate her or resent her because she got there first.'

She closed her eyes and leant back, listening to the song of the birds and the rhythmic sound of Tom's digging, and gradually the peace of the garden soothed her anguish and she fell asleep with the warmth of the sun on her face and a cold ache around her heart.

She woke to a touch on her cheek, and opened her eyes to find Tom beside her, his face troubled.

'You've been crying,' he said softly. 'I'm sorry. I've hurt you — I never meant to hurt you. . .'

She sat up. 'I'm all right,' she lied.

'No, you aren't, any more than I am.' He looked across the garden. 'I've dug over the vegetable patch — come and see.'

He held out his hand, and after a second she took it and let him pull her to her feet.

It was quite a big patch, about ten feet by twenty, and absolutely empty. 'What are you going to grow?'

His mouth quirked. 'Probably nothing. I thought I'd buy some runner beans and peas and tomatoes, and perhaps some lettuce and other salady things. I don't know, really. I don't know much about it.'

She bent and touched the soil. 'It's clay, isn't it? You'll have to work in some compost or something to break it up a bit. You want to go to a mushroom farm and get some spent mushroom compost — that's what my father does.'

'Is there one?'

'Yes, not too far away.'

'Do you know where it is?'

She smiled. 'I think so.'

'Can we go now? Have you got time?'

She laughed at his impatience. 'Yes, I've got time. You could buy the vegetable plants as well, if we see a nursery.'

'You'll have to guide me: I'm a complete novice.'

'You and me both. We'll buy a book.'

They spent the rest of the day bagging up compost

and buying little plants in trays. 'How many do I need?' he asked. Helen didn't know, so he picked up another tray of each and added them to the collection, and then sorted out three books.

'Three?'

His mouth quirked. 'I want to do it properly.'

'Why didn't I guess?' she laughed, and he paid for the things and they took them home and dug in the compost and planted the little seedlings.

Tom firmed in the last one and stood back, eyeing them doubtfully. 'It looks awfully empty,' he said.

'You followed the recommended planting distances in the books,' she pointed out. 'If you think you need more, you could always use some of these.' She waved at the left-over seed trays full of little plants.

His mouth quirked into a grin. 'We got rather a lot, didn't we?'

'Huh!' she snorted. 'Leave me out of it. *You* got rather a lot, you mean. You'll have to put them in among the flowers, like an old-fashioned cottage garden.'

'It is an old-fashioned cottage garden,' he pointed out drily, and she laughed.

'So it is. Well, then, it won't look out of place. They could do with a drink.'

'So could I,' he said with feeling. 'Let's give them a quick slosh with the hose and go to the pub.'

She pointed at her mud-stained jeans and grubby T-shirt. 'Like this?'

He chuckled. 'Perhaps not. Oh, well, I've got some wine in the fridge. How about a glass of that?'

'Done,' she said emphatically. 'I'll water the plants, you go and have a shower and sort out the wine.'

'Do I smell that bad?' he said with a laugh.

'Probably—but I'm not going to get that close,' she replied, and his expression sobered.

'No,' he said heavily. 'Right, I'll get you the hose.'

He walked away, and Helen sighed. For a while they had been able to forget, to busy themselves and work and laugh together without tension. Now, suddenly and without warning, the tension was back.

CHAPTER SIX

SEEING Tom every day at work wasn't as hard as she had imagined it would be, partly because they were always busy and so there was little time for the quiet, intimate moments that seemed to be their downfall, and partly because after that day together they had in so many ways grown closer.

They worked well together, too. Tom trusted her judgement and didn't believe in giving her endless unnecessary instructions, but on the other hand he did make sure she was in full possession of the facts on each patient so that there was no question of her misunderstanding.

His notes were clear, concise and yet complete, and he always followed through with a verbal recap to make sure nothing was missed. After that, he left the nursing care to her, respecting her professional competence, and for that she was very grateful.

Not that the others didn't, but Ross didn't trust anybody but himself, and so followed up and checked and double-checked to her distraction.

Then there came a day when he had to delegate.

He was exhausted, having covered for Tom prior to his exams more than was strictly either fair or necessary, and because the baby was up in the night and Lizzi was suffering so badly with her pregnancy he was losing out on sleep even on his nights off.

The combination was unworkable, and one Thursday morning he came in for coffee and fell asleep in the chair, slouched against the desk with a cup dangling from his fingers, halfway through a sentence.

Helen took the cup from him, put it down and went and found Tom on the ward.

'Ross is shattered—he's going to crack up if he doesn't rest,' she told him.

Tom followed her back into her office and found Ross slumped across the desk, snoring softly. He spoke his name, and when that had no effect he shook him gently.

Ross sat up with a start, looked around and rubbed a hand wearily over his face. 'Sorry, I must have dropped off.'

'Ross, go home,' Tom said firmly. 'You're not safe like this. Your judgement's bound to be affected. Look at yourself! You're shattered.'

He took a deep breath to argue, looked at Tom and Helen, and let it out again on a harsh sigh. 'How will you cope?'

'We'll cope. I've got Gavin—he's showing a lot of promise if you'd only give him some experience, and Oliver is around if anything too tricky crops up. Damn it, man, I *should* be able to cope!'

Ross's crooked smile was wry. 'Aye, you should. Sorry. OK, I'll go home and have a kip. I'll see you after lunch.

'Uh-uh. Monday, at the earliest.'

'Monday?' Ross exclaimed. 'Don't be daft! We're on call all weekend, and there are clinics this afternoon and a list tomorrow——'

'Ross, I can manage!' Tom said harshly. 'For God's sake, man, stop imagining you're the only one who's competent to do the job! At the moment, the state you're in, I should say Gavin would do better!'

Ross opened his mouth, started to speak then clamped it shut in a tight line.

'He's right, Ross,' Helen said gently. 'You know he is. You're absolutely exhausted, and if you don't get some sleep you're going to do something stupid, and you'd never forgive yourself.'

His shoulders slumped in defeat. 'OK, but I'll be at home. Any problems and I want you to call me, all right?'

'There won't be.'

'Tom —'

'OK. OK, I promise. I'll call you if I have a problem. Now go home and get to bed.'

They watched him go, and Tom shook his head slowly. 'He's just too damn conscientious.'

'At least he's gone,' Helen reasoned. 'I really didn't think he'd give in that easily. Perhaps he's more tired than we realise?'

'I think he's giving Lizzi a lot of support at home at the moment — I gather Sarah's being very demanding, and Lizzi just can't cope. He's quite worried, actually. I think he's concerned there's something not quite right with her pregnancy.'

'Who's she under?'

'Alex Carter — he told Ross the other day that she was fine, and some women just are sick. What she needs, he said, was more rest, so Ross has probably taken it to heart and is doing everything he can at home.'

'As well as everything he can here, including what isn't strictly his job.'

Tom snorted. 'Like mine, you mean? I don't know why I bothered to take my FRCS. He treats me like a houseman.'

Helen smiled. 'No, he doesn't, he just hovers like a mother hen in case you can't manage.'

'But I *can* manage, Helen, and it frustrates me that he doesn't trust me!'

'I don't think it's that,' she said thoughtfully. 'Mitch Baker was pretty grim at times, and although his previous SR, James Hardy, was very good Ross sort of got in the habit of looking over everyone's shoulder all the time. I don't think you should take it personally; he does it to me, too.'

'Yes, and I bet it irritates the life out of you!' Tom said with a chuckle.

'You guessed!'

They shared a smile, and Tom reached out his hand and cupped her cheek gently.

'Bless you for being here,' he said softly, and then he dropped his hand and walked briskly away.

It was hectic for him after that, and she saw little of him for the next two days. She was on duty for the weekend, because since she had found out about Juliette Sundays seemed unbearably long and empty knowing he was with her. It was hospital policy to have the senior ward sister on duty during normal operating hours, with less senior cover at the weekends when things were generally quieter. However, Ruth Warnes and Linda Tucker were both quite able to cover the ward during the week, and Helen now spent every third weekend on duty.

That left only two Sundays out of three to fill with busy work!

That Saturday Tom spent the day at the hospital since trade was quite brisk and it was clearly not going to be worth going home, he said. As a result he was on the ward for quite long stretches of time, chatting to his patients and making himself useful generally.

'It's wonderful not to feel I have to pick up a textbook every time I have a spare moment,' he told Helen with a laugh as they took a break for coffee. 'I feel free — it's fantastic. I even have some free time at weekends.'

She didn't want to dwell on his weekends. 'How's the vegetable patch coming on?' she asked him.

'Oh, growing like crazy. The runner beans have shot up, and the peas are flowering, and I've got a row of little lettuces that look almost ready. You must come and have a salad one night, but I should eat first, there isn't that much!'

They laughed together, and Helen thought how much happier he looked these days. Maybe it was because he had shared his burden with her. If so, she was glad, because it meant the nights she cried herself to sleep were not in vain.

Ross rang at lunchtime. 'How are things?' he asked worriedly.

'Fine,' Tom assured him.

'Are you sure?'

Helen, standing beside Tom, could hear the anxiety in his voice and smiled.

'Ross, I'm quite sure. Actually it's very quiet.'

'Oh. Right. Well, if you're sure you can manage, it's a nice day and I thought I might run up to Norfolk and bring the boys home for the weekend.'

'Do that,' Tom advised.

'I'll have my car phone — you'd better take the number — '

'Ross, just go, eh?'

There was a sigh from the other end, and then a muttered agreement.

Tom cradled the receiver and grinned at Helen. 'Worrywart.'

'He is. Don't knock it. There are plenty of consultants who just take their salary and leave all the responsibility with their teams.'

'But it has been peaceful.'

She laughed. 'Yes, it has. Poor Ross.'

But their peace — and Ross's — was about to come to an abrupt halt.

It was five o'clock and Helen was just winding up and handing over to Ruth for the evening when the phone rang.

It was Lizzi Hamilton, and Helen knew at once that something was badly wrong.

'Ross is on his way in with Callum,' she told her. 'He slipped and fell into the pool, and banged his chest against the edge. Ross pulled him out, but he went into shock —— Helen, Ross thinks he's got a ruptured spleen.'

'Oh, Lizzi, how awful — well, Tom's in the hospital, so don't worry. I'll warn Theatre to expect him and get Tom to scrub —— '

'Ross wants to do it.'

'*What*?'

Lizzi was in tears now. 'Helen, you've got to stop him! He can't possibly do it, but he's so worried — can you try and get hold of Oliver?'

Helen thought frantically. 'OK, look, I'll get Tom and Theatre organised, and get Ruth to track down Oliver if possible. But don't worry — Tom won't let Ross near him with a knife, Lizzi. I'll ring you when we've got some news.'

She put the phone down just as Tom came in, and she quickly filled him in.

'Oh, God,' he sighed. 'Oliver's gone off for the day with Bron and the kids—they're visiting relatives in Hertfordshire. I'll have to do it.'

'He won't like it,' Helen warned him.

'Tough,' Tom muttered, and she heard the steel that had sustained him through the ordeal of Juliette's coma. 'Right, ring Theatre, I'm on my way. Do you know which entrance he's coming to?'

'A and E, I would think.'

'Right, they'll know what to do. Contact them and then can you get down there and collar him? I want him out of the way as soon as that kid goes into Theatre. How old is he, do you know?'

'Fifteen, I think, or thereabouts.'

'Right. OK, I'll see you.'

'Good luck,' she called after him, and then rang A and E, warned them to expect Callum and ran down the stairs.

She arrived just as Ross pulled up outside and flung open the back door of his car. Jack Lawrence, the consultant, was there to greet them and elbowed Ross ruthlessly out of the way. Within seconds Callum, pale and semi-conscious, was on a trolley and being rushed to Theatre, with Ross beside him and Helen running to catch up.

As they swung the trolley into the Theatre doors, Tom was there, gowned and masked, ready for them.

'I'll scrub,' Ross said.

'No, you won't. I'm doing this,' Tom told him firmly, and started issuing instructions.

Callum was wheeled through into the operating-room, and Ross lunged after him.

'Get him out of my theatre,' Tom snapped, and the door swung shut in Ross's face.

'I have to do it,' he said frantically.

'Ross, don't be absurd, you aren't scrubbed! There isn't time!'

'Then I'll scrub!'

He ran into the changing-room, wrenching off his shirt as he went, and Helen followed him.

'Ross, stop!' she said firmly. 'For God's sake, look at you! You'll kill him!'

She held up one of his hands, which was trembling like a leaf. 'Look at it! What good would that be to him?'

He stared at his hand for a second, then covered his face and sank on to a chair. 'Oh, God, Callum, please don't die,' he whispered raggedly.

Helen sat beside him and hugged him. 'He'll be fine. He's still alive, Ross. They'll be through the wall by now and Tom will have that artery in his hand. The blood's on its way, and they will have cross-matched him already. He'll be fine.'

As she said it, she just hoped it was true. A major rupture would pour blood into the abdomen so fast that there was often little that could be done unless action was taken almost instantly.

Hopefully, because Ross was so alert Callum had been brought in in time. However, there were no guarantees, and Helen found the time dragging endlessly.

A nurse, gowned and masked, appeared in the doorway. 'They've halted the bleeding. Tom's taking his spleen out now.'

As the tension drained out of him, Ross seemed to

collapse under Helen's arm. 'Oh, thank God,' he murmured unsteadily.

The nurse's eyes smiled over the mask. 'Don't worry, Ross, he's going to be all right. They'll be some time sorting him out, so why don't you go and get a coffee and we'll let you know how he's getting on in a little while?'

Helen stood up. 'You'd better put your shirt back on,' she said gently. 'I'll get some coffee and see you outside. We can wait up here.'

While she poured the coffee Ross gave Lizzi a quick ring, and promised to call her as soon as Callum was out of Theatre.

'How long can it take, for God's sake?' Ross muttered over and over again.

It was nearly an hour later before Tom came out, still gowned, and smiled wearily at Ross. 'He's OK; I've closed him up and he's just gone through to Recovery. He's going to be OK.'

Ross smiled awkwardly. 'Thanks.' His face crumpled and he turned away, biting his lip. 'Hell—sorry,' he muttered, and Tom rested a hand on his shoulder and squeezed.

'Don't worry about it. Do you want to go through and see him?'

He nodded, and Tom led him away. Helen sank back against the chair and heaved a sigh of relief. How she'd stopped Ross going into Theatre she just didn't know, but she was heartily relieved that she had.

Tom was, too. He rejoined her a few moments later, sank on to a chair beside her and took the cup from her hands, draining it at a gulp.

'Would you like more?'

He gave a fleeting smile. 'Would I! My God, what a

mess. His two lower ribs were caved in and his spleen was split neatly in half. It's a good job Ross didn't wait for an ambulance; he wouldn't have made it. I nearly lost him as it was.'

Helen handed him a cup. 'It's a good job you didn't.'

He met her eyes, his own touched with humour. 'Ain't it just! God, what a day.' He blew out his breath on a long sigh and tipped his head back. 'Thanks for keeping him out of the way.'

She snorted. 'It wasn't easy. I expect a reward.'

He gave her a crooked grin. 'Done. Come for supper one night next week, and I'll do you something with a home-grown side salad.'

Her heart leapt, then settled to a steady thunder. She had thought she'd got her feelings for him under control, had managed to maintain a platonic relationship with some success. Now she found out to her great dismay that she had had no success at all, that it had simply been a lack of exposure to him in a personal setting that had made her self-delusion possible.

'I'm not sure that would be a good idea,' she said softly.

'Just a meal, Helen. Nothing more.' His voice was coaxing, and his eyes were shadowed with loneliness.

It was that more than anything else that made her agree.

'No strings, I promise,' he assured her. 'We can handle it.'

She wondered if he really believed it, or if he was fooling himself, too.

Callum improved steadily overnight and by the time Helen came back on duty on Sunday morning he was much stronger.

He had been put in the little single room by the

nursing station and Ross had spent the night in the chair beside him. His transfusions of whole blood were now complete and he was on a saline drip with antibiotics and pain-relief IV.

His ribs were giving him some pain, and the bruising was horrific.

'That's one colourful tum you've got there,' Helen said with a smile.

Callum's mouth tipped in a sideways grin identical to his father's. 'Yeah. If it didn't hurt it would be fine. Listen——' He beckoned her closer, and she bent over him. 'Get Dad to go home, could you? He's dead beat and he will stay here, and I know he needs to sleep.'

Helen studied the young face, and saw maturity beyond his years in the clear grey eyes. 'He thinks you need him.'

'Yeah—in one piece. Please try, Sister. Lizzi's really worried about him. I think that's half the reason she's feeling so sick.'

'Who's feeling sick?' Ross asked from behind her, and Helen turned and pushed him out of the room.

'Come, I want a word.'

She led him into the office and told him Callum wanted him to go home. 'He's all right, Ross, and frankly he could do with some peace to sleep this off. He's worrying about you, and that isn't going to help his recovery. Why don't you go home and get some rest?'

Ross glowered at her. 'Why don't you stop interfering?'

'Because I care,' she told him candidly. 'You're making yourself ill and that doesn't help any of us. Now stop being belligerent and go home.'

'Belligerent? I like that! Just because I'm here looking after my son——'

'No, you aren't! You're here fussing over him like an old hen. We're looking after him, or trying to, and what he needs is rest. Savvy? Rest. Now are you going to co-operate, or am I calling Tom?'

'Calling Tom for what?' Tom asked from behind her.

'He won't go home and Callum's fretting about him.'

Tom ran his eyes over Ross's exhausted face and shook his head slowly. 'Ross, you are shattered. He's fine, really. He's going to be perfectly all right, but he does need his sleep and the last thing he wants is to have to worry about you.'

Ross sighed shortly. 'Who's the boss round here anyway?' he grumbled, and then shot them a grin. 'Sorry, I'm just. . .'

Tom flung an arm round his shoulders and gave him a brotherly hug. 'I know what you are just—overly conscientious. Now go home, and come back this afternoon with Lizzi to see him.'

Tom ushered him out, then came back in and grinned at her. 'Impossible, isn't he?' I wonder what it will take to stop him?'

'God alone knows. A ten-ton truck?'

Tom chuckled. 'Very likely. When are you coming for supper?'

Her mouth went dry.

'Whenever you like—any night during the week.'

'Tuesday?'

She nodded. 'Fine.'

'OK. Right, I have to pop down to A and E—they've got a query appendix just come in. I'll see you later.'

* * *

She was on a half-day on Tuesday, and spent the afternoon shopping. As soon as she had come off duty she had glanced through her meagre collection of clothes, felt uninspired and decided it was time to enlarge her wardrobe.

Nothing whatsoever to do with Tom, she told herself, but everything was at least two years out of date apart from the leggings and T-shirt she had worn several times before.

Not, of course, that it mattered what she wore. It was a simple matter of self-respect.

She bought a softly flowing shirt in cotton lawn sprawling with huge pastel flowers on a navy background, and a loose, short-sleeved navy cotton sweater to wear over it, and then some more cotton slip-on shoes and another T-shirt.

She saw one in fuchsia-pink and picked it up, then remembered it was Juliette's favourite colour and put it back, her buoyant mood shattered.

What did it matter what she wore, anyway?'

She showered and put on the minimum of make-up, then wore the new skirt and jumper simply because it was stupid not to, but she found she wasn't really looking forward to the evening any more.

Tom was in the garden when she arrived, wandering round with a pair of secateurs in one hand and a handful of roses in the other.

'Hi — am I on the drag or are you early?'

She smiled faintly at him. 'I'm probably early. Sorry.'

'Don't worry. Come on in and have a drink. I'll just put these in water.'

She followed him into the kitchen and watched as he struggled with the roses.

'Ouch! It got me!' he muttered, sucking a finger, and she smiled.

'You have to snip the thorns.'

'You're telling me! Evil things. Look at that!'

He held out his finger, and she watched a tiny bead of blood well out of the skin. 'Ah—poor baby! Want me to kiss it better?' she teased.

He hesitated, then dropped his hand. 'Yes, I do, but I think you'd better not,' he said in a tight voice.

She sighed and set down her glass. 'Oh, Tom, what are we doing?'

He stopped fiddling with the roses and stood still, staring out of the window. 'Going crazy? I've tried, Helen—I've tried so hard. I went and saw Juliette last night. She was asleep, and she looked almost normal. Then her eyes opened and she stared straight past me. I might as well not have been there. I thought, Why am I doing this? Why don't I just do what everyone expects and divorce her and get on with my life? But I can't, Helen. I know it's stupid, and I know it's pointless, but as long as she's alive I have to be there.'

'I know—Tom, it's all right, I understand.'

'But it isn't all right!' he said in a harsh whisper. He turned to face her, and his eyes were filled with despair. 'I want to be with you, to hold you, to make love to you, to go to sleep with you and wake up with you by my side. I want to share my life with you, and I'm being torn in half——'

He broke off and held out his arms, and she flung herself against him and hugged him hard, unable to bear it any more.

For a long time he simply held her, then she felt his lips brush her temple, then the side of her jaw, then the hollow of her shoulder.

'You look very pretty tonight,' he murmured, and his lips trailed on, over her collarbone and up, round her jaw, over her eyelids and down across the other cheek. 'You smell wonderful,' he muttered gruffly, and then his hands slid lower and eased her against him. She stiffened, then moaned softly and pressed against him, desperate to eradicate the space between them.

'I want you,' he breathed, his voice harsh with desire. 'I want to hold you, and feel your softness all around me, and bury myself in you—I need you, Helen, I need you. . .'

She thought her knees would buckle at the sudden wash of sensation that flooded her. She wanted him, too—needed him, needed to feel him close to her, part of her—but never hers.

With a soft cry she pulled away. 'Tom—stop. Think what you're doing!' she pleaded.

He stared at her, his eyes glazed, and then his lids fluttered down.

'I'm sorry,' he said gruffly. 'Damn, Helen, I never meant—— Forgive me.'

She backed towards the door. 'I'd better go ——'

'No! Helen, please, don't go now, for God's sake! I promise I won't touch you. Please. Don't leave me alone.'

She looked at him sharply, and saw the strain etched deep in his face.

'Are you all right?'

He laughed, a heart-rending sound that tore her apart. 'No—not really. I'm at the end of my tether, Helen. I need someone to talk to—not about anything in particular, but just to be part of the human race again. Does that make any sense?'

She sighed heavily. 'Yes, it makes sense. It makes

sense to me, at any rate.' She looked around the kitchen for something to do, and found the roses. 'Shall I do these for you while you get the supper?'

The tension eased out of him fractionally. 'Yes — thanks. We'll eat outside.

'Fine.'

He carried the things out while she snipped the rose thorns and arranged the blooms in a bowl, then set them on the kitchen table.

There was one red one, which didn't really go with the others, and she put it in a champagne flute and ran upstairs to put it by his bed.

There, on the table she and Tom had bought together, was a framed photograph of a beautiful girl with long, glowing auburn hair.

Juliette.

Helen felt her heart contract, and the pain was like nothing she had ever felt before.

It seemed inappropriate to leave the rose beside the picture, so she took it downstairs and put it in among the others. So what if it didn't go? It was better there than upstairs, adding fuel to an already explosive situation. God knows it was difficult enough for them to keep their distance without any further encouragement.

She made her way out to the garden and found Tom and the food under the trees. He had bought a set of teak chairs and a table, and as she crossed the lawn he stood up and smiled.

'OK?'

She nodded. She wasn't, far from it, but nothing was to be achieved by rubbing it in.

He passed her the salad bowl. 'Home-grown lettuce.'

She peered into the nearly empty bowl, and smiled. 'I don't think it was quite ready,' she told him.

His mouth quirked. 'Probably not. Never mind, there's plenty more. Here, have some cold chicken.'

She helped herself and reached for the tomatoes. 'Home-grown?' she asked with a little smile.

'Of course — and the cucumber!'

Their eyes met in a smile of understanding. No, they couldn't have what they wanted — at least not all of it — but they could still share some time together, and all that self-denial had to be good for the soul, Helen thought wryly.

If only there were an end in sight. . .

CHAPTER SEVEN

HELEN didn't see Tom again except professionally for nearly two weeks after that night.

He was busy covering for Ross, who naturally was spending time with Callum whenever he could, and they seemed to be unbelievably busy.

There was a youth of about Callum's age who had had his appendix out, and Helen put them together so that they could keep each other company. Callum's ribs were more painful than his incision, although Tom had wired them after he had removed Callum's spleen, and he found his chest physiotherapy very painful. Ross, however, explained that now his spleen was gone he was more susceptible to infection, particularly chest infection, and so despite blockbuster antibiotic therapy would need to keep his chest as clear as possible.

And so he gritted his teeth and co-operated, and Helen had to admire him for his guts.

He was a lot like his father, quick-witted, funny, and very compassionate. Helen liked him, and found herself quite often chatting to him if things were quiet.

'I'm going to be a doctor,' he told her one day about ten days after his admission.

'Good. I think you'll be a good one, but hopefully you'll take it slightly less seriously than your father.'

Callum grinned. 'He's better now. Lizzi's been nagging him and he's eased off on the coffee.

'I'd noticed. I wonder why?'

'Oh, his heart does funny things if he's had too

much, and Lizzi panics,' he said matter-of-factly. 'She says she doesn't want to be a widow again, and then he lays off it for a bit. He's OK.'

Helen found that bit of information very interesting, and mentioned it to Tom.

'Oh, yes, he gets the odd ectopic beat when he's been overdoing the coffee. Nothing drastic, but he is aware of his heartbeat occasionally doing funny things. So Lizzi's nagging him, is she? Good for her. Perhaps it will stop him hammering on till he gets a heart attack!'

Helen frowned. 'Do you think that's likely?'

He laughed. 'No, not at all. He's got more sense — I think! Lizzi has, anyway, by all accounts.'

'I gather she's also feeling less sick, and Sarah's started sleeping better.'

'Three cheers all round!' Tom said with feeling. 'Look, are you doing anything on Saturday?'

She was instantly wary. 'Why?'

'There's a traction-engine rally near here. I thought it might be fun. Fancy coming?'

She did, but not because of the traction engines. She hesitated for a second.

'Please?' he asked coaxingly. 'I don't really want to go on my own, but if you'd rather not we could go somewhere else. What do you fancy?'

You, she thought absently, but that was a fruitless train of thought.

'The traction engines would be fine,' she told him, and was rewarded with a fleeting smile.

'Thanks. I'll sort out the times and let you know more later in the week.'

Helen wondered if it might not be a very grave

mistake, but then an emergency put all thought of her personal problems right out of her mind.

A man had fallen asleep at the wheel, and his delivery van had run off the road and a section of timber fencing had rammed through the cab and impaled him, finally coming to rest in the bulkhead behind the seat.

An emergency team headed by Jack Lawrence rushed to the scene, and Ross and Tom both scrubbed and were waiting when he was admitted, the timber cross-member still projecting from his abdominal wall.

It was a long, tricky and extremely hazardous operation, and twice they nearly lost him, Tom told her afterwards, but finally he was down from Recovery to ITU and the following day he was moved to the little single room next to the nursing station.

His name was Peter Seager, and he was married, in his early twenties, and his pregnant wife was beside herself with worry.

Helen sent her off for some lunch and a little walk in the grounds to freshen her up and blow the cobwebs away, and also to give Helen herself a little light relief.

She was specialling him herself, because he was still very critically ill, although now more stable. His large bowel, small bowel, right kidney and liver had all been damaged, although there had been remarkably little damage to major blood vessels.

Only one, the renal artery, had been torn, and that had been compressed by the timber and thus held firmly shut until they removed it. Having survived the threat of immediate haemorrhage from that, the most serious damage had been to his small bowel, and a large section had been removed completely. Otherwise it had been a question of removing the huge quantity of debris from his abdomen together with all the bowel contents which had been discharged into the peritoneal cavity, and cleaning him up as well as possible before reassembling the abdomen into some sort of semblance of normality.

Tom and Ross had worked side by side on him, and Gavin Jones, the SHO, had been deeply impressed to watch them working.

'They're brilliant,' he told Helen. 'If I get to be a tenth as good I'll be amazed.'

She looked up from the chart she was completing and smiled. 'Tom's very complimentary about your operating.'

'He is? Good God.'

She chuckled. 'You're too modest for your own good.'

'Maybe.' He wandered off, his step jaunty, and Helen smiled. All he needed was his ego boosting.

A few minutes later he was back. 'Have you seen Callum today? I'm not too happy—he's supposed to be going home later but he apparently had a slight temperature at ten and I'm a bit worried about him.'

'How is it now?'

'It's still up—only a degree, but even so. . . I wonder if we ought to put him back on antibiotics?'

'Ask Mr Henderson—he's technically in charge, because Mr Hamilton can't be, but that doesn't mean he's had a look-in!'

Gavin went and a short while later Oliver popped his head round the door. 'Hi. Just put young Hamilton on to penicillin again. He's spiked—could be just an upper respiratory, but it could go on to his chest and we can't be too careful now he's lost his spleen. Have you seen Ross?'

'He's in Theatre,' she told him.

'I'll pop up and let him know. Don't think it's anything to worry about, but we'd better be on the safe side.' Oliver came further into the room. 'This the chap who got run through?'

'The very same. He's doing quite nicely in a rather sorry sort of way.'

'I'll bet he's sorry,' Oliver said with a twitch of his eyebrows. 'Poor bloke—I gather Ross and Tom were amazing.'

She laughed softly. 'You've been talking to Gavin.'

He smiled. 'You guessed. He's got a serious case of self-doubt, that young man.'

'Mmm. What he needs is to be flung in at the deep end—a weekend on his own, or something.'

Oliver snorted. 'You volunteering to be one of the guinea pigs?'

'I thought you said he suffered from self-doubt?' she protested.

'He does,' Oliver agreed. 'It doesn't necessarily mean it's unfounded, though. What he needs is for Ross to stand beside him with his hands tied behind his back and tell him what to do. He's altogether too ready to snatch the scalpel and do it himself!'

'Poor old Ross,' she murmured.

'Poor old Ross is fine,' Oliver said with a snort. 'He could just do with being more of a consultant and less of a do-it-yourselfer, otherwise no one else will ever get a look-in!'

'Well, why doesn't someone tell him?' Helen asked, eyeing him levelly.

'Someone like me, for instance?'

She laughed. 'You guessed!'

'More than my life's worth. I'm still trying to work

out how Tom kept him out of Theatre when he
operated on Callum!'

Helen raised her eyebrows. 'Tom? *I* kept him out —
and let me tell you, he wasn't impressed!'

Oliver chuckled. 'I can imagine! Right, I'll go and
get on with my clinic — give my SHO enough rope to
hang herself! Let me know how Callum does. He'd
better stay in until tomorrow at least, I think, just to
be on the safe side.'

She turned her attention back to her patient, Peter,
who was drifting in and out of consciousness. Just then
he opened his eyes and she bent over him, smiling.

'Hello! How are you feeling now?'

'Hurts,' he mumbled. 'Everything — hurts.'

'OK, I'll give you a bit more pain relief. Would you
like your mouth washed, as well?'

He nodded slightly, and after giving him a little more
Pethidine from the pump she sent Susan, the third-year
student, for a mouthwash trolley.

'Do you want me to do it?' she asked.

'No, I'll do it,' Helen told her. 'You go and carry on
with the obs.'

She cleaned up his dry, caked lips and sponged his
tongue, then took a swab and ran it over all of his teeth
in turn.

'Better?'

'Mmm — fresh. Thanks.'

'You're welcome. I'm just going to check your
drains.'

'Sound like a plumber,' he said with a tiny stab at
humour, and Helen laughed softly.

'That's me — keep all the tubes in working order.
That looks lovely. Well done. I'd like to turn you in a

minute, so you don't get sore. I'll just get someone to help me.'

Susan had finished doing the observations and Helen called her over. 'I want to turn him—could you give me a hand? I'll get Ruth as well, because we need to do it smoothly.'

Together they lifted him towards the edge of the bed, moved all the drains and suction apparatus to the other side of the bed and carefully turned him over.

He moaned with pain, and Helen smoothed his damp brow and apologised.

'It'll hurt less and less as time goes on,' she promised him, but it must seem a distant prospect to Peter, she imagined.

His temperature was up, and he was clearly suffering from acute peritonitis, an expected complication because of the length of time the peritoneum had been contaminated before they were able to clean him up. He had been trapped for two hours before they managed to free him by cutting the van to pieces, and that coupled with the splinters of fencing hadn't helped at all.

He was lucky to be alive, but she doubted very much if he would agree at that moment.

His wife came back, and she looked a little better. Helen moved the easy-chair to the other side of the bed so that she could see him, and popped out to have a look at Callum.

'Keep an eye on Mr Seager, could you?' she asked Ruth who was working at the desk, and then went into the next bay where Callum was lying listlessly in bed.

He felt hot to the touch, and was clearly not feeling at all well.

'Do you hurt anywhere?' she asked.

'My chest, a bit,' he mumbled, and put his hand over his collarbones. It was reassuringly high on his chest, but Helen wasn't taking any chances.

'OK, I'll get Mr Henderson back to have a look at you later, after the antibiotics have had a chance to work. Did you tell him your chest hurt?'

'It didn't then,' he told her.

'Oh. OK, well, I'll ring him. He's in a clinic, but I suppose he ought to know.'

'Where's Dad?' he asked her, and he sounded like a little boy again.

'Operating. He'll be down to see you soon, I expect.'

She went into the office to call Oliver and tell him about the chest pain, and just as she finished the call Ross came in, still in Theatre greens.

'How's Callum?' he asked shortly.

'Temperature's rising and he's got a bit of upper chest pain—I've just called Oliver.'

'Pneumococcal pneumonia—damn. I had a feeling this would happen.'

'He's on penicillin already, and I was just on my way to get a sputum sample. Perhaps you'd like to do that?'

'Sure.' She took him to the CSSD store, found him a sputum cup and sent him off.

'Giving him something to do?' Tom asked from behind her.

'Oh, hi—no, actually Callum's got a slight infection. Ross thinks it's probably pneumonia.'

'On, no! Poor kid. Is he OK?'

She shrugged. 'Very early. I'm sure he will be; he's already on penicillin and it should knock it on the head quite fast, but he looks pretty floppy.'

He inclined his head towards the single room. 'How's Count Dracula?'

Her brows creased in a frown. 'Count Dracula?'

'Yes, you know, the stake through the heart routine.'

She spluttered with laughter. 'Pretty ropey. He's running a temp and he's in a lot of pain.'

Tom nodded. 'He will be; he's got raging peritonitis. We'll have to watch him for a liver abscess, I think. Any bile draining from the wound?'

She nodded. 'A little, I think. Not very much.'

'Hmm. Well, watch that too. I'll come and have a chat to him. Oh, about Saturday, by the way — I'll pick you up at eleven, if that's OK.'

'Saturday?'

'The traction engine rally?'

'Oh — yes, of course. Sorry, I'd forgotten it was this Saturday, what with all the upheaval. It's been a bit chaotic.'

'It has a bit, hasn't it?' he said, and she wondered if she had imagined the look of hurt in his eyes. If so, it was unfounded. It was merely the date that had slipped from her attention. Tom Russell and his day out were very much in the forefront of her mind.

Callum's fever proceeded to rise during the course of the afternoon, but by the following morning it had levelled off and was slowly coming down again.

It turned out to be nothing more serious than a slight upper respiratory infection, and by the afternoon he was much better, more like his perky old self.

'I thought for sure he'd got pneumonia,' a very relieved Ross said later on that day.

'Yes, he was lucky,' Helen agreed. 'If he hadn't been so co-operative about his chest physio he might well have developed it anyway. When are you taking him home?'

'Tomorrow, now. Oliver's on call so I can spend the

weekend with him. Maybe I'll drum some sense into him about running round the pool!'

And I, Helen thought with a tingle of something she didn't want to analyse, will be spending the day with Tom.

Saturday dawned bright and clear, a lovely hot June day with a light breeze to take the edge off the heat, and Helen showered and dressed in a giddy mixture of anticipation and dread.

She wore a light T-shirt over her jeans, and comfortable trainers for a change because there would inevitably be a lot of walking around. It wasn't the most feminine combination, and in a little gesture of defiance she gave herself a quick spritz of body spray and a flick of lipstick to redress the balance.

Tom was on time, and she was relieved to see he was in jeans as well, looking far too sexy for her peace of mind. He smiled briefly, and her heart jerked in her chest.

Will it ever stop that? she thought in desperation. They drove slowly through the country lanes with the sunroof open, and with the sun on her face and the wind in her hair she felt suddenly carefree.

She would forget about Juliette today, about her love for Tom and his deep sense of honour, and just concentrate on having some light-hearted and harmless fun. God knows they both deserved it.

They arrived at the rally and parked in a field, then joined the crowd thronging towards the entrance. Already she could hear the barrel-organs and the carousels, and the steady hiss of steam punctuated by the occasional whistle. The air was tinged with the smell of smoke and steam, and as they moved between the huge and colourful engines Helen was glad of her thin T-shirt and the slight breeze.

'Hot, isn't it?' Tom said in her ear. 'Look, what a beauty!'

They admired the engines, with their huge iron tyres and massive wheels, the polished brass and gleaming coachwork, and on each one a smutty, red-faced enthusiast stoked the fires and polished the trim and answered questions with a smile.

'Do you know much about them?' Helen asked Tom, and he shook his head.

'Nothing — it just sounded colourful and rather fun.'

'It is — they're works of art really, aren't they?'

'Monuments to dedication — the love lavished on them must be unreal.'

She though of Juliette, of Tom washing her hair every Sunday, brushing it till it gleamed.

'Are you OK?' he asked softly.

She forced a smile. 'Yes, I'm fine.' How foolish to think she could forget, even for a few hours.

'I'm hungry,' he told her. 'Let's get something to eat.'

They found a hot-dog stand and munched as they wandered among the engines, and then they found all the little working engines, the pumps and the ones that drove conveyors and lathes and other workshop equipment.

'Aren't they gorgeous?' he yelled over the noise.

'Tiny monuments,' she said laughingly, and refused to be sad.

He took her hand and led her through the crowd, and somehow they ended up still holding hands hours later.

'How about a go on the funfair?' he asked.

'I get sick when things move too fast,' she told him, and he promised to find something gentle.

They went in the swing boats, and then on the magic carpet, and finally the carousel, Tom sitting behind her because the ride was almost full.

She was desperately conscious of his thighs behind hers, his chest against her back, his arms that reached round her to grasp the pole and coincidentally brushed her sides.

She heard his laugh in her ear, and he ducked his head away.

'What's the matter?' she asked, and he grinned.

'Your hair keeps blowing in my face — it tickles.'

She put one hand up to contain it, and seconds later his lips brushed her knuckles.

'OK?' he asked, his warm breath teasing her ear, and she felt her heart kick.

'Wonderful!' she said with painful honesty, and his arm came down and circled her waist, holding her firmly against him as the ride picked up speed.

'Hang on!' he laughed.

She forgot her hair, forgot everything except clinging on for dear life — and Tom, close behind her, keeping her safe.

When the ride stopped he helped her down and took her hand.

'OK?'

'My knees have gone!' she confessed with a laugh, and he put his arm round her waist and held her against him.

'Better?'

'Much.' If her heart could stand the strain.

She followed unresisting as he led her between the

engines with their glowing fire-boxes, and on to the car park.

'Have you seen enough?' he asked, almost as an afterthought.

She nodded. In truth, she didn't feel she could bear the bittersweetness any more.

It was cooler now in the early evening, and he drove back to the cottage and pulled up in the drive.

'I thought we could have something to eat — round off the day,' he said.

Helen, who had thought the day was ending and that she would be relieved, found her spirits lifted at the prospect of another few hours in his company.

They made supper together — more salad from the garden, and some wafer-thin honey roast ham and smoked turkey breast that he found in the fridge, and hot, crisp bread rolls from the freezer finished off in the oven.

They ate it in the kitchen, both of them ravenous after all the fresh air, and then they made a cup of tea and took it down the garden, sitting on the bench under the apple trees.

When he had finished Tom stretched out on his back on the ground and patted the grass beside him.

'Lie down here with me and look at the stars,' he said softly.

She hesitated.

'Please?' he said softly. 'I want to talk to you, and I can't do it with you up there and me down here on my own.'

So she lay beside him, but not too close for the sake of her peace of mind, and for a while he just stared up at the night sky.

'Tom, what's wrong?' she asked gently after a while.

He sighed. 'Us. This whole crazy situation. Wanting you, needing you the way I do, and knowing there's nothing I can do about it. I just wish I knew what Juliette would want. Once, the time I rescued her in Marrakech, she asked me to promise her that if she died I would find someone else and get married and have children — all the things that we had planned. I told her not to be maudlin, but I think she was serious. After we came back she went to a solicitor and made a will, and I've often wondered if she knew something was going to happen.'

'Maybe it was just being sensible,' Helen said carefully. 'Perhaps it was realising, as you do in medicine, that we aren't immortal. I mean, we always think it won't happen to us, but it happens to someone every day. There are no guarantees. Perhaps she realised that.'

He sighed heavily. 'Perhaps. Anyway, it was only a few months later that she had the accident.'

It was a hard question, but she had to ask it.

She turned her head towards him but it was too dark to see more than the outline of his face.

'Do you ever wish she had died?'

'Oh, God, Helen, don't ask me that. I don't know. There were times when I wished she had, times when I was glad she hadn't and that I still had her, no matter how remote she seemed. That's why I visit her, and talk to her — how do we know what's going on in her head? My mind says nothing, but my heart wonders if she's trapped in there, all alone, just waiting for my visits. That's why I can't abandon her. I might be the only ray of light in a living hell.'

In the darkness his hand reached for hers and clung. The silence was softened by the song of birds and the quiet rustling of the night. She could hear him breathing, feel the beat of his heart under her thumb as it curled against his hand.

Where did he find the strength to stand by Juliette with such devotion? From his love for her?

Helen felt pain stab through her, the bitter, fruitless pain of jealousy.

'That's what you're like for me,' he went on softly. 'A ray of light in the darkness. Sometimes I dream I'm struggling through a barren wilderness, all alone in the dark, and then in the distance I see a light. When I get nearer, I can see it's a campfire, and you're sitting beside it. For some reason I can't join you, I have to sit outside the ring of light in the darkness, but just knowing you're there somehow helps, as if I'm not quite alone. Then the fire goes out, and I can't see you any more, and I wake up crying your name.'

She shifted closer to him, unbearably moved by the sadness in his voice, and he wrapped his arms round her and cradled her head against his shoulder.

'Where do you draw the line, Helen?' he asked raggedly. 'At what point am I being unfaithful to Juliette? If I make love to you? Or before, wanting to, thinking about it in the long hours of the night? Am I being unfaithful when I wake up in the early hours, aching for you? I can't help it, Helen. I've tried — God knows I've tried — but I can't help wanting you, needing you, longing for you. . .'

He turned her face to his and kissed her, his lips urgent, demanding, and she opened her mouth to him and slid her arms around his neck, drawing him closer.

He dragged his mouth from hers, his breathing unsteady, and pressed his lips against the pulse in her throat. 'Stop me, Helen,' he pleaded, over and over, as he laid hot, open-mouthed kisses against her throat.

She tried to push him away but he wouldn't go, holding her still, his mouth returning to hers in desperation. She could feel the emotion raging in him, the need and the pain, the craving to love and be loved, and the endless, aching loneliness.

A sob rose in her throat, and he lifted his head, resting his brow on hers as his breath gusted raggedly against her face.

'Oh, Helen, forgive me. I'm sorry — what am I doing to you? Oh, my love. . .'

His arms slid round her, holding her against his chest while she wept for his courage, and his pain, for a love that could never bloom — and for Juliette, trapped all alone in the dark.

CHAPTER EIGHT

THAT Sunday was the longest day of Helen's life. It was also the hardest, because it was on that day that she decided her relationship with Tom must end.

There were many reasons, not least of which was her concern that in the end they would weaken, and his infidelity, so far only involuntary and spiritual, would become a physical reality.

Knowing what that meant to him, she thought it only fair to avoid it if at all possible, and there was no doubt that these harmless, so-called platonic outings they kept inventing did nothing to lower the heat in their relationship.

Another reason, this one very personal, was her knowledge of herself. There was no way she could ever have a physical relationship with Tom without it destroying her own self-respect — or at least not while Juliette was alive.

So far their relationship, while it had brought Helen pain, had been justified in terms of offering friendship and support to Tom during a very difficult time. Now, though, that very relationship was adding to his troubles, and the easiest thing to do was to end it. It was also the most difficult.

On a professional level, of course, they were to a certain extent forced into contact, but they had proved that they were able to keep their feelings under control in those circumstances.

It was only when the circumstances changed and they

were alone that things grew too difficult, so she
resolved, after much heart-searching, never to allow
him to sweet-talk her into another potentially inflam-
matory situation.

They had parted on Saturday night with bittersweet
regret, and Helen wasn't sure how Tom would behave
to her on the Monday morning.

She needn't have worried. They were so busy that
there was little time for conversation. Peter Seager—
Tom's Count Dracula—was very unwell. He had
developed a high temperature, despite his antibiotics,
and he had an area of extreme tenderness over his
liver. It was almost certainly the abscess that Tom had
feared, and they decided to scan the liver to see if they
could locate the source of the infection.

Sure enough, there were three abscesses, clustered
around the site of the injury. He was taken to Theatre
and the abscesses aspirated with a long needle, using
ultrasound to guide Tom to the infected pockets. The
sites were then flushed with antibiotic, and by the
afternoon he showed slight signs of improvement.

'Just hope it holds, or we may end up having to open
him again to do a more drastic clean-up,' Tom told her
later when he came to the ward to check the man's
progress.

They were alone in the office and Helen was winding
up her courage to tell him that she couldn't go out with
him again when the phone rang.

It was Bron Henderson, passing on a complicated
message for Oliver. While she was jotting the message
down Tom waggled his fingers at her, winked and went
out.

So, she had missed an opportunity to tell him of her
decision. Oh, well, it wasn't as if he had suggested

another date. Perhaps he wouldn't. Perhaps Saturday
had been enough to convince him, too, that their
relationship was untenable.

'Sorry, Bron, could you say that again?'

She forced herself to concentrate, and by the time
she put the phone down Tom was off the ward and had
gone down to help Ross out with his clinic.

The next day was just as busy, with Tom in and out
and Helen coping without Ruth, who had a cold.

Ross was working shorter hours—in fact just his
normal rostered hours—as Callum was still at home,
which meant that Tom's workload increased and he
was consequently too busy to think about time off.

As far as Helen was concerned, it couldn't have
come at a better time. It would give them a cooling-off
period after last Saturday, which could only be a good
thing.

One other person appreciated the change—Gavin
Jones, Ross's SHO. He was perforce given more
responsibility, and he handled it well. Tom was very
impressed by his thorough history-taking in clinics, and
the quickness with which he spotted potential compli-
cations with the patients.

'He's going to be a very good doctor,' Tom told
Helen in a rare quiet moment.

'Make sure you tell him that,' Helen said. 'I get the
feeling it's all he needs.'

Jack Lawrence, too, spoke highly of Gavin's cool-
headedness with patients admitted to A and E, and
Helen saw his confidence increase by leaps and bounds.

The weekend after the steam rally Helen went away
to stay with her parents in Hereford, and arrived back
on Sunday night to find a note under the door:

'Thought you might like to come for lunch today (Saturday). Ring me if you get back in time. Tom.'

Well, she thought, one good reason to have gone away.

She went into work on Monday to find Tom already in evidence.

'Hi — where were you?' he asked with a smile.

'I went home to my parents for the weekend.'

'Oh. Just wondered. Did you get my note?'

She nodded. 'Yes — sorry, I wasn't back until late last night and I didn't think there was any point in ringing and waking you up.'

In fact she hadn't been back that late and had almost rung him — had even picked up the phone a number of times — but he didn't need to know that.

'What brings you here so early?' she asked instead.

'Emergency I'm tacking on to the beginning of the list,' he told her. 'Appendicitis — young woman of nineteen. Gavin admitted her last night and kept her in for observation. Apparently she's got classic symptoms — pain in the right side of her abdomen, rebound tenderness, colic — even Gavin couldn't miss it! I'll whip it out first thing. The night sister will tell you all about her.'

Jean Hobbs, their usual night sister, had the weekend off and was being covered by an agency nurse. She gave Helen a sketchy report, and then left on the dot of eight.

Helen, irritated by the lack of commitment and concerned about the paucity of information, went round the ward herself checking charts, chatting to patients and generally trying to fill in the gaps.

Karen Hudson, the girl with appendicitis, was looking pale and listless. As Tom said, her temperature was

normal, but her respiration was fast and light, and she
certainly looked very unwell.

As Helen spoke to her she moaned softly and curled
up, clutching her abdomen.

'Very sore?' Helen asked, and she nodded.

'Oh, awful. It comes in waves. . .'

She moaned again, and Helen smoothed her hair
back. 'Poor love. Is there anyone we can call for you?'

She shook her head. 'No. No one. My parents are
miles away — I'll ring them when it's over and tell
them — there's no point in worrying them now.'

'No boyfriend?'

She shook her head again. 'I've only recently moved
here — I was in Norwich before. Well, we split up so I
thought it was a good time to go — ow — oh, help, it
hurts. . .'

Helen squeezed her hand. 'Soon be over. You're
going up to Theatre as soon as you've had your pre-
med.'

After dealing with that and making Karen's bed after
she went off to Theatre, Helen went in to see Peter
Seager.

He was making good progress now following his
abscess drainage a week before, and Ross was hopeful
that he would continue to do so. He was able to get up
and sit in a chair now, and was surprisingly cheerful
considering the magnitude of his injuries.

He had nothing but praise for the treatment he had
received, and Helen was touched by his kindness. It
was men like him that made her job worthwhile.

It was a good job someone did, she thought just a
short time later, because there were others that were
just a fruitless waste of time.

Karen Hudson was back from Theatre, without her

apparently perfectly healthy appendix. According to Tom there was nothing inside her to indicate any reason for her pain and rebound tenderness, and Ross was on the warpath.

Who had diagnosed appendicitis, and why? he wanted to know.

Gavin's neck was firmly on the block.

Ross gathered the whole team — Tom, who had performed the operation, Helen, who had prepared Karen for Theatre, and the unfortunate SHO who had diagnosed it and admitted her.

'Right,' Ross said tightly. 'I want a blow-by-blow account of every word exchanged with that girl, every symptom described, every physical change detected, and I want to see every scrap of paper with any relevance to her case — and I want it *now*!'

Helen left to retrieve the notes from the end of the bed, and called up the records on the computer, running a print-out.

By the time she went back into her office Gavin was halfway through the story of her admission.

'Definite rebound tenderness——'

'That's dead easy to fake.'

'The rapid pulse isn't,' Gavin protested.

'If you're on an adrenalin high from anticipation and the threat of discovery, as she probably was, then you don't *have* to fake it!'

Gavin was adamant, though. 'It was there, nevertheless, and it fitted. Everything she said was right — absolutely everything. It started with a loss of appetite, she had apparently vomited once, her pulse-rate was up, the pain started, she said, in the centre and spread round and down to the lower right quadrant. There was a choice, I thought, between salpingitis, mesenteric adenitis and appendicitis. The history fitted appendicitis best.'

Ross swivelled his eyes to Tom. 'What about other possibilities?'

Tom shook his head. 'No, from what I could see there was nothing else wrong. It looked a normal, healthy abdomen. Her ovaries and fallopian tubes showed no sign of cysts or inflammation, there was no evidence of any mesenteric inflammation, her bladder and ureter looked quiet — nothing. I did check, Ross, believe me.'

'So what conclusion did you come to?'

Tom shrugged and raised his eyebrows.

'Quite.' Ross turned back to Gavin. 'It looks very much as if you have committed one of the cardinal sins of surgery, young man — you have caused an operation to be performed on a perfectly healthy young woman — '

'But I could have sworn there was something wrong — '

'There is! I'll lay you odds she's got Munchausen's syndrome — basically, lad, you've been suckered. You've all been suckered,' he said in disgust.

Tom shook his head and sighed. 'Ross, believe me, she was very convincing. You would have made the same diagnosis yourself.'

'Nobody can fake it that well or consistently,' Ross argued.

'Oh, they can — they do! How do they end up with so many scars?'

'Another point — didn't that alert you, Gavin?'

Gavin shook his head. 'There were no other scars. She hadn't had any operations.'

'Well, she has now,' Ross said heavily. 'And if she

has got Munchausen's and she's got no scars, you can bet your life she's under age. How old did she say she was?'

'Nineteen,' Helen told him. 'She could well be younger — or older. It's very hard to tell at that age. Ask a pub landlord.'

Ross glared at her. 'How did she get past you?'

Helen sighed. 'Ross, she was entirely convincing! She's articulate, middle-class, likeable — she even said she didn't want to worry her parents!'

Ross snorted. 'I'll bet! Right, I want you to get on to the police. Missing persons — did she say anything about how long she'd lived in the area?'

Helen felt her heart sink. 'Not long. She said she'd come from Norwich. She'd split up with her boyfriend and it seemed a good time to move,' she told them heavily.

'Typical — they flit like butterflies. Right, ring the Norfolk and Norwich, speak to A and E, find out if they've had a girl answering her description — they will have either rumbled her or had her in for observation and sent her home again — and go through all her possessions with a fine-tooth comb. There might be some clues there.'

He stood up and headed for the door. 'I want to know the minute she's awake enough to talk — I want a word with that young lady about wasting Health Service resources — and the rest of you, I suggest you get back to work and start earning your keep!'

He stormed out, leaving Tom, Helen and a very subdued Gavin to discuss the case.

'Do you suppose her parents will sue me?' Gavin said worriedly.

Tom laid a reassuring hand on his shoulder. 'No. It's

my neck on the block, because I examined her and performed the operation. You merely pointed her in my direction. And anyway, if there's any suing to be done it'll be of her, for the wasted resources—talking of which, we have a lot to do today. Come on, don't worry, I was suckered too. And if it's any comfort, Ross would have been, I'm sure.'

Gavin snorted, but went off to carry on with his work.

Helen blew out her breath. 'She was very convincing. I'm still not entirely convinced she made it up.'

Tom shrugged. 'It's beginning to look more and more likely. Get on to the police and the Norfolk and Norwich—in fact, all the hospitals in the area—and see if there's a pattern. Let me know what you find out.'

'OK,' Helen said amiably. 'If you give me a mobile phone I'll see if I can fit in any nursing while I'm at it.'

Tom met her eyes and a brief, rueful smile touched his lips. 'Have you got any other ideas?'

'Ross's secretary? She's efficient, she's got the contacts and she's probably got the time at the moment, because he's put off his private work until Callum's better.'

'Right—try her. Better check with Ross first, though—don't want another crisis!'

Ross, however, was instantly agreeable. 'Good idea—you haven't really got time, I know that. Give Sheila a good description, if you can. That was my only reservation, that she hadn't seen her, but if you can give her enough information I'm sure you'll sort something out.'

So Helen contacted Sheila, his secretary, gave her

all the information she could, and then went back to work.

Ruth was agog. 'What was all that about?'

'Munchausen's — Karen Hudson. Either there's nothing wrong and she needs an Oscar, or Tom didn't find the cause of the problem.'

'Ouch! So whose head's going to roll?'

Helen laughed. 'Everyone's, I suspect. Come on, help me go through all her things.'

They emptied her locker, spread the contents of her bag out on the desk in the office and discovered some very fascinating and conflicting things.

'She's called Katrina Harrington.' Ruth waved a girocheque.

'Not according to this.' Helen held up a passport. 'According to this she's Katherine Hoole, and she's seventeen.'

'Well, which is most likely to be correct?'

'The passport,' Helen said without hesitation. 'When I got one I had to send my birth certificate and all sorts of things. No, I reckon we've got her.' She reached for the phone. 'Sheila? It's Helen Cooper. We've found a passport — name of Katherine Hoole. Run that by the police. She's seventeen, but we don't know where she's from. Oh, hang on.' Ruth passed her a tattered envelope, and she pulled out the letter. 'There's an address here in Norfolk, headed paper — the letter's signed "Mum". could you pop down and have a look, then call the police? We'll need to let them know.'

An hour later Sheila rang her back. 'You were right. The police have been in contact with her parents. Seems she left home about three months ago, and lived in Norwich for a while. They lost contact about seven weeks ago. The Norfolk and Norwich turned her away last month—told her she'd have to bone up on her medical if she wanted to fool anybody. She's obviously been doing that—— Oh, and by the way, Dad's a doctor.'

'Surprise, surprise,' Helen sighed. 'They often are. Thanks, Sheila.'

Ross came down to the ward a short time later. 'I've spoken to Sheila—I gather the parents are on their way. I'll talk to them before I talk to Karen—sorry, Katherine.' He sighed heavily. 'I am not looking forward to this inverview one iota,' he confessed. 'If someone had done this to one of the boys——'

He sighed again. 'Oh, well, I suppose I should be thankful for small mercies. At least my kids are just plain idiotic, not hell-bent on self-destruction like this lassie. I'll see you later.'

He left again, and Gavin emerged from one of the bays looking wary.

'Has he gone?' he asked quietly.

She smiled reassuringly. 'Yes, Gavin, he's gone. Look, don't worry. Her parents are coming in and Ross is going to talk to them. I suggest you keep out of the way.'

In the event it appeared that Katherine had been trying to con her father for years. She had registered with another practice because she wasn't getting enough medical attention from her father, and had trotted backwards and forwards over the past three years with endless aches and pains and imaginary ills.

'She can be extremely convincing,' her father assured Helen as they stood at her bedside. 'I shouldn't blame yourselves; she conned me a few times until I realised what she was up to. Too clever for her own good. I used to find her curled up on the settee with my medical books. I hid them in the end, and she got less accurate.' He gave a wry laugh. 'Oh, well, she's got something real to worry about now. Perhaps that'll put her off, silly kid. I'm sorry she's put you all to so much trouble.'

Gavin's relief was almost palpable. So was his astonishment when Ross apologised. 'If she can fool her father, she can fool a total stranger. I'm sorry I went off the deep end. Incidentally, Gavin, that was a very thorough history you took from her. Well done. I'll be mentioning it in my report to the management committee.'

Helen thought she was going to have to scrape him off the floor when Ross had gone.

It was too much for Tom, and he sagged against the wall and laughed till the tears ran down his face. 'Oh, Gavin, your expression's priceless,' he told the bemused young man. 'Helen, give him a cup of coffee, I think he deserves it!'

Katherine progressed rapidly, although she suffered quite severely from distension and wind-pain in the first forty-eight hours. Helen expected Ross to take the attitude that it served her right, but he was actually quite genuinely sympathetic.

'I don't want to be too nice to her and give her the impression that it's a good idea, but she is a likeable young lady,' he confided in Helen on Friday morning. 'And entirely plausible. I can quite see how you all fell for her. She's very knowledgeable. Perhaps she ought to have "Munchausen" tattooed on her tummy to warn future surgical teams.'

Helen laughed. 'Then she'd need an operation to remove the tattoo!'

Ross chuckled. 'Wretched child. Her parents are taking her home this afternoon. Perhaps she'll settle down for a while. At least we won't see her again here.'

'No, they're a bit like lightning, aren't they? They never strike twice in the same place. Could you have a look at Peter Seager while you're here? He's complaining of abdominal pain again, and I thought I could hear an increase in bowel sounds.'

Ross sighed. 'Adhesions? Or another abscess?'

Helen grinned. 'You're the consultant — you tell me!'

He shot her a wry grin. 'OK, point taken. I'll examine him myself!'

Ross decided to watch him closely over the next few hours, and by lunchtime it was obvious that something was badly wrong. Peter was vomiting, and in increasing pain, and he seemed to be becoming distended. He was also slightly constipated and Helen felt Ross ought to see him again.

He appeared with Gavin, and examined the patient again, listening with a stethoscope for bowel sounds.

'Yes, there's a lot of activity in there. What happens,' he told the patient, 'is that if scar tissue develops after surgery, sometimes it can constrict the bowel or get tangled round it. Now it looks as though this may have happened, and your bowel is trying to free the obstruction by working overtime. Hence all the colicky pain and the vomiting. Now, what I'd like to do is take you back up to Theatre and free those bands of scar tissue, and then we should soon have you feeling more comfortable.'

Peter nodded miserably. 'I don't care what you do just so long as it stops hurting.'

'OK, Sister, we'll take him up shortly. If you could

prepare him and give him the pre-med, we'll get that sorted out this afternoon.'

He wrote up the drugs on the chart, hung it back on the end of the bed and left with Gavin.

'One for you, I think,' he said to the SHO as they walked away.

And that's a turn-up for the books, Helen thought in surprise. He must think something of him if he'll let him tackle this.

She changed Peter into an operating gown, gave him his pre-med and stayed with him until the Theatre porter came with the trolley.

As they left, Dr and Mrs Hoole arrived.

'Hello. Have you come to take Katherine home?' she asked with a smile.

'Yes. I'm sorry about all this,' her mother said. 'Look, I wonder if you'd do something for us? There are one or two things in this bag—little thank-yous for the people who were put out. Could you make sure they get to the right sources?'

Helen took the bag, which was surprisingly heavy for one or two 'little thank-yous'. 'How kind—yes, of course I'll make sure they get them. Thank you very much.' She put the bag down on the desk and looked across to where Katherine was sitting chatting to another patient. 'She's all ready for you. I think she's actually quite looking forward to coming home.'

'We're looking forward to having her,' her mother said feelingly. 'We've missed her, the minx.'

Helen watched as they collected all their daughter's things, and then on the way out Katherine surprised her by giving her a hug.

'I'm sorry I was such a pain,' she confessed.

'Just don't do it again—surgery can be so dangerous.

It's bad enough when you need it, never mind when you don't.'

Katherine lifted her shoulders in a helpless shrug, and Helen watched them go, her heart heavy. Hopefully the girl had learned her lesson, but it was unlikely. More probably she had used her stay in the ward to glean information from other patients to add to her repertoire.

What a sorry mess.

Peter Seager returned to the ward after an hour, and Gavin came down to tell Helen all about it.

'He'd got bands of scar tissue round his ileum—it must have been very painful. One of the loops had twisted, as well—probably because of the vomiting, Ross said—and he was very distended with wind. Anyway, I managed to free all the adhesions, and hopefully he'll be better, but I can tell you I was terrified about making a mess of it. I mean, I've closed for him before, but never done the whole thing. I think it'll take all weekend to get over it!'

Helen chuckled. 'I'm sure you were fine. Is Ross coming down?'

He shook his head. 'Not yet. He's got paperwork to do and he wants to get off early. He said he'd pop in before he went home. Why?'

'We've got a bag of goodies from Katherine's parents. There's something for him in there—and you. Do you want to go and have a look? They're on my desk. I don't know what they are; they're all wrapped and labelled.'

She finished settling Peter, and after checking that he was comfortable and programming Susan, the third-year, to give him a wash she followed Gavin.

'What have you got?'

'A bottle of wine — a very nice one. I think Tom has, too. What's this?'

He picked up Ross's parcel. It was flat, floppy and about half an inch thick and six inches square.

'I don't know — I thought it might have been a compact disc, but it obviously isn't.'

'Not unless it's a floppy disk!' Gavin quipped.

'Oh, very droll. Ah, Ross, there you are. Present for you, courtesy of the Hooles.'

'Me? Really?' He picked it up and felt it, then stripped off the paper. 'It's a book — *Medical Emergencies — a pictorial glossary of terms and conditions*, by Mitch Baker — well, I'll be damned!'

He chuckled and opened the book, and within moments he was laughing helplessly.

'What is it?' Helen asked.

'A paralytic ileus,' he chuckled. He handed her the book of cartoons. 'You won't remember, you weren't on this ward then, but it was just after I started. We had a patient, a woman, who ended up with an ileus because Mitch was a bit quick on the draw giving her solids. That's me in the cartoon, propping up the ileus.'

Helen peered at the cartoon, then at Ross. 'He's good — it's an excellent likeness.'

'Too damned excellent — give me that back. I might ring the young rip up and ask for some royalties, seeing as I star in it.'

Tom came in, and Helen handed him his present and explained.

'Wow — good stuff,' he said when he had opened the wine. 'Oh, well, it's always welcome. What did you get?'

'A box of Belgian chocolates, and another box for the rest of the nursing staff. Aren't they kind?'

Ross nodded. 'Very nice people. I feel extremely sorry for them. I don't think this is the end of it, by any means. Right, I'm away home. Cheerio, everyone. Have a good weekend.'

Gavin glanced at his watch. 'I'm off duty in an hour! Yippee! I wonder what Ruth's doing tonight? Perhaps she'd like to share this bottle of wine.'

He left, and Tom smiled tentatively at Helen. 'Sounds like a good idea — got any plans for this evening?'

She opened her mouth to tell him that she didn't think it was a good idea at all when there was a tap on the door and the third-year stuck her head round. 'I've finished with Mr Seager — what would you like me to do now?'

'Uh — I don't know. Hang on, I'll be with you in a tick.'

The girl left, and immediately the phone rang. She answered it despairingly. 'Surgical — Sister Cooper — oh, hello, Kath. No, Oliver's on this weekend. Right. OK.'

She cradled the receiver. 'Right, where were we?'

'I asked you if you had any plans for tonight.'

She hesitated a second. She really needed to talk to him at some length, not just simply say, I don't think we should see each other. And tonight would give her the ideal opportunity.

'No, none. Let me go home and sort out one or two things, then I'll come over.'

'Then you can't drink.'

'No, and it's your wine, so that's really the fairest way. I tell you what, I'll bring my chocolates, and then you needn't worry about me.'

He laughed, a low, unconsciously sexy laugh that

tingled round her senses and made her wonder if going round to his house alone was such a good idea after all—even to tell him that it was the last time.

It could, she feared, be the straw that broke the camel's back.

CHAPTER NINE

WHEN she pulled up outside his house, Helen found Tom in the garden, watering the vegetables.

'Hi. Come and see.'

'Gosh, they look fantastic!' she exclaimed. 'Well done.'

He grinned fleetingly. 'Beginner's luck. Guess what's for supper?'

'Um—let me hazard a guess. Salad?'

He chuckled. 'Got it in one. Come on, let's go inside; the insects are out for my blood.'

They went into the cottage and he poured her a glass of the wine the Hooles had given him. 'Here, it's lovely stuff. I've already started, I'm afraid.' He snorted. 'Dutch courage.'

'Dutch courage?' She looked at him searchingly. 'Why would you need Dutch courage, Tom?'

He looked at her, then down into his glass, swirling the contents thoughtfully. 'I wanted to talk to you. The wine was just a good excuse—I've been wanting to talk to you for a couple of weeks, actually, ever since the traction-engine rally, but there just hasn't been time.' He gave a hollow laugh. 'Ironic, really. I wanted to talk about us spending time together and whether we really should, and it's been totally irrelevant because we've been too busy, even if we'd wanted to!'

She laughed softly. 'I've been wanting to talk to you, too—about the same thing.' She sighed. 'Never mind, I'm here now. Do you want to kick off?'

He shook his head. 'No, you start. Tell me how you feel.'

She shrugged slightly. 'Confused? Perhaps slightly less so now, in that I think I've got one of the answers. You asked me, that day, where the line of infidelity was drawn.'

'And?'

She met his eyes candidly. 'I think we have to draw it ourselves. I think, really, we both know where it is.'

His smile was brief and sad. 'I have to be able to live with myself, and go and visit Juliette without feeling a heel. I'll miss you, though.'

'You'll still see me — there's work.'

'Yes — but it's not the same as spending the day with you, holding your hand and desperately pretending to myself that it's all right.'

He set his wine down, removed her glass from her fingers and pulled her into his arms.

'I've tried so hard not to want you,' he murmured softly. 'I really didn't want to hurt you, and yet I couldn't leave you alone. But it's the only way, and we both know that. I'll miss our expeditions and meals and shopping trips, though.'

'Me too.'

His arms tightened, and she slid hers round his waist and hugged him hard.

'Oh, Tom. I'll still be here to talk to, you know. You can always lean on me when things get too much. That hasn't changed.'

'Are you sure?' he asked her quietly, holding her away so that he could look in her eyes. 'I can offer you nothing, Helen — not even hope.'

His face was concerned, but his eyes held a sort of wild desperation. She couldn't abandon him now.

'I'm sure,' she told him, her voice ripe with conviction. 'I'm not in this for what I can get out of it, Tom, but I'll always be here for you. Always, no matter what, however rough it gets. Remember that,' she said fervently.

'Bless you.' He pulled her back against his chest and hugged her, then let her go. 'I suppose we should eat something, and then I ought to send you home.'

She gave a tiny, rather sad little laugh. 'Yes, I suppose so.' She took a deep, steadying breath and stepped away from him, out of danger. 'What can I do?'

They prepared the meal together, trying hard not to brush against each other in the small area by the sink.

Once Helen turned and Tom walked straight into her, reaching up automatically to steady her.

They were touching, their faces mere inches apart, and the sudden flare of need in Tom's eyes set her on fire.

She looked away, away from the eyes that would be her undoing, suddenly aware of the dripping lettuce in her hand. 'Excuse me,' she muttered, and picked up the salad-spinner from the table, whirling the lettuce round with rather more force than was necessary.

'Don't take it out on my poor lettuce,' Tom said softly, and her shoulders slumped.

'It's so damn difficult,' she wailed. 'I just want to be in your arms. . .'

The tears started to fall, and Tom drew her back against his chest and murmured soothingly in her ear.

She pulled away. 'We're crossing the line again, Tom,' she told him desperately. 'This isn't going to work.'

'Yes, it is. Sit down, I'll get the supper. You have

another glass of wine and relax, and try and forget I'm here.'

She gave a strangled snort of laughter. 'Fat chance,' she said hysterically. 'Could you put a bodybag on, or something?'

He chuckled softly. 'That's better. Now, more wine, and sit and do nothing—or, better still, go and play the piano.'

'I can't!' she protested.

'You can. Anybody can. Doing it well is the difficult thing, and I still can't. Go on.'

She went through to the sitting-room, now comfortably furnished with their junk-shop finds, and sat herself at the piano.

It was ages since she had played, and she flexed her fingers and tried to play a piece from memory. Her memory, however, proved defective. She tried another piece and gave up in despair.

'Oh, hopeless!' she laughed.

Tom, behind her, chuckled. 'OK, I believe you; you need practice.'

'Pig.'

'I only agreed with you.'

She stood up and turned to face him, trying to keep a straight face. 'Yes, well, it wasn't very gentlemanly. If you're so good, let's hear you play.'

'After supper. Come and eat, it's ready.'

He had grilled some steaks, and together with the salad and hot rolls it was a wonderful meal.

'Oh, I'm full!' she declared finally, pushing her plate away.

'You never finish anything.' He speared the last mouthful of her steak and ate it, then picked up his wine glass. 'Come on, then, you wanted to hear me make mistakes on the piano.'

She followed him, laughing, and sat in one of the chairs facing him while he seated himself on the piano stool and flexed his fingers.

'What sort of thing do you like?'

'Anything. Amaze me.'

He did. He played some Beethoven, a few Scott Joplin rags, something from the *Mikado*, and then a haunting melody in a minor key that almost reduced her to tears again.

After a while he stopped, his head bowed.

'Don't stop,' she said softly. 'It's beautiful.'

'Enough's enough.' He put the lid down, then came and sat opposite her, his face thoughtful.

'What's wrong, Tom?' she asked him, sure that she knew the answer.

His smile was sad and didn't make it to his eyes. 'I used to play for Juliette. I'd forgotten what it was like to have an audience.'

She regarded him steadily for a second, then stood up. 'I think it's time I went.'

He searched her eyes, and nodded. 'You're probably right.'

'I'll let myself out.'

She walked past him, and as she did he lifted his hand and caught her wrist gently, lifting her hand to his lips. 'Thanks for understanding,' he murmured.

She turned her hand and cupped his cheek, treasuring the feel of his face—the roughness of the stubble against the smooth skin beneath, the solid feel of his jaw under her fingers, the soft fullness of his lips against the pad of her thumb.

'You're welcome. I'll see you on Monday.'

She eased her hand away and walked quickly out, before she did something stupid to spoil it all.

It wasn't easy, but then they never imagined it would be. However, nature was on their side, and so they were mercifully busy with an unseasonal flush of emergencies.

In the middle of July Tom went to London, for the diploma ceremony at the Royal College of Surgeons. The night before he went he took Helen out for a drink and they sat in a crowded bar and could have been alone.

'I wish I were able to come tomorrow,' she told him.

'Why?' he asked. He sounded absolutely amazed.

'Because it's an achievement,' she said frankly. 'You worked very hard, and you've been justly rewarded. I would just like to see that being publicly acknowledged.'

He flushed and laughed self-consciously. 'You're silly.'

'No, I'm not. Juliette would be proud of you, Tom,' she told him with conviction. '*I'm* proud of you.'

'Oh, Helen. . .' He took her hand, clearly choked, and gave her a fleeting, quirky little smile. 'You funny girl,' he murmured, but his voice was still slightly strangled.

'I'm not funny—just honest,' she told him.

Their eyes locked for an age, then he glanced at his watch. 'Come on, drink up; I have to get my beauty sleep if I'm not going to look dreadful in the photos.'

She chuckled. 'You think sleep's going to make a difference?'

'Miaow,' he said, and the tension eased a little in their laughter.

He took her home and she leant over and kissed his cheek. 'All the best for tomorrow. I'll be thinking of you.'

'Thanks.'

She climbed out of the car and walked to the door, conscious of his eyes on her, and as she opened the door and turned to wave he tooted and drove off. She watched him go, her heart still with him, and let herself back into her empty flat.

She made a cup of tea and curled up in front of the television, but there was a weepy film on and she couldn't watch it. Instead she went to bed and lay wondering if this was all life had in store for her, to spend mock-platonic evenings with the man she loved, and then come home — alone.

Peter Seager was finally well enough to be discharged, a success story that they should all have been proud of. His wife, now very pregnant, was touchingly grateful.

'I brought you all some chocs, just to say thanks,' she told Helen.

Helen was touched. 'That's very kind. He's been a lovely patient.'

She smiled fondly at him. 'He's a lovely man. I can't thank you enough ——'

She broke off, choked, and Helen patted her on the shoulder. 'Go on, take him home and look after him.'

'Oh, I will,' she said fervently. 'I will.'

One of their previous patients, however, had fared less well.

A few days after Peter's discharge, Judy Fulcher was re-admitted with knife wounds to the abdomen and thighs.

The police this time pressed charges themselves, and

her husband was remanded in custody on a charge of causing grievous bodily harm with intent to murder.

Judy was rushed to Theatre where Tom struggled to save her, and finally with Gavin's help he was able to stem all the bleeding and start the slow job of repairing the damage.

She went to ITU for the first two days, then was transferred back to the ward, pale and very subdued.

'Hi there,' Helen said, perching on the chair by her bed. 'Didn't expect you back — how are you feeling?'

Judy rolled her eyes. 'Sore. I thought I'd just got over all that — I was feeling so much better, but — well, I've met someone, you see. We haven't done nothing, but — well, he found out about it.' Her shrug spoke volumes.

'Oh, I am so sorry,' Helen said, taking her hand. 'That's dreadful.'

'They said I was lucky to survive last time, but this — well, I tell you, Sister, when he was coming at me with that knife I thought my number was up.'

She started to shake, and then her eyes filled with tears. Helen squeezed her hand. 'That's right, you have a little cry, get it out of your system. It must have been a terrible experience.'

She looked up to find Tom watching her, his eyes thoughtful.

'Do you want to see her?' she asked quietly.

He shook his head. 'No, it's all right, let her cry. I'll come back later.'

He went into the office and she watched him go. It had been a week since the diploma ceremony, and she missed him dreadfully. Seeing him at work was somehow different, and she longed just to be with him.

If only they could keep their feelings under wraps, and just enjoy being together. . .

On Saturday she found she couldn't face another day alone. She set off in her car, with no particular destination in mind, and ended up at Tom's cottage.

He was just locking the back door when she turned in to the drive, and he came over to her and leant on the car roof, looking in through the window.

'Hi. Everything all right?'

'Yes—I suppose so. Just another endless day off.'

He laughed without humour. 'I was just going for a walk. Come with me.'

So she locked the car and they set off down the track beside the field, and then cut across to a little river that meandered sleepily through the fields.

'This is lovely.' She took a deep breath of the fresh country air, and sighed. 'Birdsong, the drone of bees and tractors—you are lucky.'

He grunted, and she looked keenly at him.

'Tom, what's wrong?'

He snapped off a blade of grass and threw it in the river, watching it as it swirled away on the surface. 'Oh, nothing. Everything.'

They walked on a way, and then he stopped by a grassy bank.

'Do you feel like listening?'

'Yes—sure.' She sat down and patted the grass, and he stretched out beside her and plucked another blade of grass and chewed it for a moment.

'It's Juliette,' he said abruptly. 'I was there the other night, talking to her—absolute rubbish, mostly. I told her about the diploma ceremony again, and about Judy being stabbed and what a bastard her husband is, and I suddenly thought, if she can hear me, is this what she really wants to hear? She can't switch off, or tell me to go away, or ask questions. Probably it's all irrelevant, because I doubt very much if she's registered a solitary word I've said to her in the past three years, but if it isn't. . .'

He trailed off and sighed heavily. 'I never thought I'd want her to die, that I'd look at her and wish it were over, but I did the other night. I don't know — my thinking gets all confused, and I wonder what the spirit is, what it is that makes us who we are, and when that spirit leaves our body — always assuming that we are more than just a collection of synapses firing randomly to make some sense of the world.'

He pulled a leaf off the bush beside him and shredded it absently, clearly miles away. Helen watched him without moving, reluctant to disturb his train of thought, happy simply to let him pour it all out.

'I wonder what it's like to be her, to be trapped in there,' he continued quietly. 'If she is, she'd hate it. She never sat still for a moment, and her mind was always whirling — she was exhausting to be with, like a beautiful hyperactive butterfly, constantly flitting from one thing to another but somehow managing to achieve a huge amount. To be idle was anathema to her, and I just hope to God her consciousness is as low as they say it is.'

He went quiet for a minute, shredding another leaf. 'You know, if it weren't for her parents I think I might have asked them not to feed her any more, but they're clutching at straws still, hoping they'll get her back. And anyway, I don't feel I can really examine the issue dispassionately, because my judgement's clouded by love. I wouldn't trust myself. All I know is I don't want to see her suffer any longer. We wouldn't let it happen to a dumb animal, so why Juliette? Oh, God, Helen, I don't want her to die but I just wish it were all over!'

He threw down the scraps of leaf and jumped up, striding away from her, his face bleak.

So he did still love Juliette. She had wondered about that, and now she knew.

The pain wasn't as bad as she had feared. After all, she knew Tom better now, and she would have been more surprised if he hadn't loved Juliette any more.

Her heart ached for him. He was just as trapped in his way as Juliette, only he was aware of what was going on, and the moral choices open to him. It must be intolerable.

Her heart heavy, she got slowly to her feet, brushed the grass off her jeans and followed him. He was waiting for her a little further on, sitting on a fallen tree, and he gave her one of those quicksilver smiles that made her heart flutter.

Only today it didn't, because she saw the pain and anguish behind the mask, and instead she wanted to weep.

Judy Fulcher continued to make progress, and one of her most frequent visitors was the man who had precipitated the latest row with her husband.

He was small, a quiet, unprepossessing man, but with a wealth of kindness in his eyes.

'I just feel safe with him,' Judy said one day after he had left. 'He reminds me of Dr Russell—he's the sort of man you marry, because they won't let you down. Do you know what I mean?'

Helen did, indeed, know what she meant. She thought how surprised Judy would be if she had any idea how accurate her statement was.

'It's Mr Russell now,' she told Judy instead. 'He's become a Fellow of the Royal College of Surgeons since he first operated on you.'

'Promotion, eh? Seems a shame to throw away the "Doctor", though—I always think it sounds so romantic!'

Helen laughed. 'I know what you mean. Right, I must get on, I'm off duty now and I've got to catch the shops.'

She drove home and walked round to the corner shop, buying a few essentials, and then walked back to find Tom on the doorstep.

'Hi. Thought I'd take you out for supper.'

She couldn't help the smile of welcome. 'Oh, you should have rung. I've just bought some stuff—and anyway, I thought we weren't going to do that any more?'

'Just a pizza—nothing romantic. Or we could go to the cinema. I'm just sick of the sight of my four walls.'

She looked at her shopping, and weighed up the pros and cons.

'Oh, to hell with it. Come in and have something quick, and we'll go to the cinema. Do you know what's on?'

He shook his head. 'Got a paper?'

'No—I read the patients'. It's cheaper!'

He chuckled. 'You're useless. Tell you what, you throw something together and I'll nip round to the shop and get one.'

But the shop had sold out, so after they'd eaten they went to the cinema anyway and chose the most likely-looking of the three obscure films that were showing.

It was a poor choice. It turned out to be a passionate film about a couple who were condemned to be apart, and it was punctuated with tasteless but none the less powerful love scenes that did nothing for Helen's peace of mind.

After a particularly torrid scene Tom nudged her arm. 'Come on, let's get out of here. I can't stand any more of this.'

They walked back to her flat, and on the doorstep she turned to him.

'Are you coming in?'

'After that lot? Helen, I wouldn't dare.'

His eyes burned bright, and her heart kicked against her ribs. She could still feel the warmth running through her, the aftermath of the love scene they had witnessed, and wanted nothing more than to duplicate that scene with Tom.

She stood on tiptoe and kissed him softly. 'Goodnight, Tom. Sleep tight.'

She turned away and let herself in, shutting the door behind her without a backward glance.

She didn't dare look. A bit like Lot's wife, but she felt she would turn into a pillar of fire.

They tiptoed round each other warily for the rest of the week, both heavily conscious of the passion boiling just beneath the surface.

Helen had thought it would go away, but clearly the images were too strong, and her mind replayed the love scene again and again, substituting her and Tom for the characters on the screen.

Her sleep was fragmented, and her waking hours were a living hell because Tom seemed to be there every time she turned round.

On one occasion they found themselves alone in the office, and their eyes met and blazed.

'I want you,' he said baldly.

'I want you, too.'

'Hell, isn't it?' He laughed softly. 'Damn film. I can't get it out of my mind.'

She smiled ruefully. 'Neither can I.'

His bleep squawked, shattering in the silence, and he picked up the phone and rang the switchboard.

'A and E,' he told her, and then turned his attention back to the conversation. After a brief exchange, he hung up.

'Emergency?'

'Perforated duodenal ulcer, judging by the sound of it. I'll go and check. Have we got a bed?'

She nodded. 'Yes, two of Oliver's patients went home today.'

'Good. Right, I'll go down. See you later.'

She watched him go, tormented by her feelings, and wondered how much longer they could both go on.

There was little time for idle speculation, however, because there was another emergency admitted while Tom was still in Theatre, and Gavin was called out of Ross's clinic to make arrangements for her admission.

She was young, healthy and had appendicitis—and Gavin was terrified.

'Help me!' he pleaded, his eyes wide. 'Has she or has she not? Helen, I can't cope!'

She laughed. 'Gavin, get out there and function. Of course she has! Not even you are so unlucky you could have another Munchausen's!'

'Oh, God, I hope you're right,' he sighed, and, taking a deep breath, he went back into the ward to continue clerking the patient.

Ross finished his clinic and came up, and after examining the girl was quite satisfied that she had a bona fide appendicitis.

'Unless she's drawn a hot red patch on the right side of her abdomen, she's for real,' he said drily. 'I'll do her once Tom's out.'

'Why not let Gavin follow it through?' Helen suggested softly.

'Teaching me my job?'

She grinned, not the least afraid of him. 'You've told me mine on occasions.'

He sighed shortly, then laughed. 'OK, you win. Gavin can do it — but I'll be there.'

'Fine. No one was suggesting you should abandon him to his own devices!'

'Abandon who?'

'Oh, hello, Tom. Gavin, but I'm not. How's the DU?'

He looked tired. 'Oh, all right, I hope. It must have perforated to some extent some while ago, because there were adhesions to the gall bladder and pancreas, but now he's perforated with a vengeance and he's got a roaring peritonitis just to jolly things along.'

Helen tutted. 'Why don't any of them get to the doctor sooner?'

'Indigestion,' Ross said in disgust. 'I think indigestion remedies are the cause of more major problems than anything else we have to deal with. If people weren't led to believe that indigestion was normal, they might pay more attention to their excruciating pain before their ulcers perforate! Oh, well, I'd better get Gavin under way on this young lady, I suppose.'

Tom frowned at the door as it closed behind Ross. 'Young lady?'

'Appendix.'

His eyebrows twitched. 'Is she for real?'

'You too?'

He laughed. 'I don't think any of us will forget it in a hurry. Now, this new guy—name of Adrian Butcher. Here are his notes. I'd better fill you in before he comes down from Recovery.'

They stayed on opposite sides of the desk, but their heads were together, and she was conscious of the way his hair grew, the texture of his skin, the slight shadow of stubble on his jaw. He had just showered, and she could smell the soap on his skin. It drove her wild.

'Leave it here, Tom, I'll read it,' she told him breathlessly.

He met her eyes and smiled ruefully. 'Yes, OK. I'll go away and let you concentrate.'

But she couldn't, because the fragrance of his skin fresh from the shower lingered on the air, and even his bold, jagged writing conjured up his image.

It was an impossible situation, and it seemed to be getting steadily worse. She wondered how they could possibly go on.

They didn't have to. On Sunday night the doorbell rang, and she opened it to find Tom standing there, his face a rigid mask.

Cold shivers of dread ran over her. 'Tom—what is it?' she asked.

'Juliette's dead,' he told her harshly. His voice sounded as if it didn't belong to him, and he was trembling.

'Oh, dear God—come in,' she told him, and stepped back, but he shook his head.

'No—I have to get back to the clinic and see if I can find out what happened. She was fine when I left at four, but when I got home the police were on the doorstep——'

His voice cracked and she dragged him in and wrapped her arm round him, steering him to the sitting-room.

'Tell me all about it.'

He shrugged helplessly. 'That's all I know. One minute she was alive, and the next — Helen, I have to go.'

'Sit down and have a drink first — tea or coffee or something.'

He shook his head. 'No, I'm all right, really. The policewoman made a cup of tea. It was just seeing you. . .'

He wrapped his arms round her and hugged her tight, his face buried in her hair, and she rubbed her hands against his back and held him, trying to take away the hurt.

After a few moments he straightened and gave her a bleak smile.

'I'll keep in touch — don't wait up; I doubt if I'll know anything tonight.'

She watched him go, full of misgivings, and eventually went to bed. She didn't sleep, though. It was a development she had schooled herself not to expect or hope for, and now it had happened she didn't know what to feel.

She went to work in the morning and found Ross in her office.

'Oh, Ross, I'm glad you're here,' she said with relief.

'You may not be,' he told her heavily. 'Tom's father rang. Tom's at the police station in Norwich, apparently, helping the police with their enquiries. Apparently Juliette's parents weren't satisfied that she died of natural causes. They think Tom murdered her.'

CHAPTER TEN

HELEN was stunned. Murder? Tom?

'It's ridiculous, of course,' Ross said gruffly. 'There's no way Tom would do anything like that.'

Helen met his eyes bleakly, a terrible suspicion taking root in her mind.

'Not even if he loved her enough?'

Ross held her eyes. 'You think he could?'

She shrugged. 'I don't want to think he could, and I'd deny it to the bitter end, but he's been under terrible strain, Ross — for years.'

'And he's found you now, of course.'

She shook her head. 'No. No, he wouldn't do that just for me, so we could be together. That's not the sort of man he is.'

'But for Juliette?'

She shrugged. 'He was never convinced that she was as inert as she seemed. That's why he talked to her so much, why he washed her hair every Sunday and wouldn't let them cut it. He said she was like a beautiful hyperactive butterfly. Maybe he just wanted to set her free — '

Her voice broke, and Ross pulled her into his arms and held her while she cried.

It was a hot item, of course, for the local evening papers, and even the national dailies were interested — which meant that from shortly after ten that morning they were hounded by the Press. The hospital security staff did their best, but the reporters seemed to ooze out of the woodwork and pop up in the most unlikely places.

Finally the hospital management committee called a Press conference at midday, and issued a statement saying that they had no reason to suspect Tom of any unethical behaviour. He had always followed a very strict code of personal conduct with regard to his work, and there was no question in their minds that he was innocent. Certainly none of the patients at the hospital need have any fear for their safety.

But the Press were after blood, and somehow got hold of the fact that Tom had been seeing Helen.

She was taking down a drip when a reporter appeared at her elbow.

'Sister Cooper? I'm from the Anglian *Evening Standard*—I wonder if you would mind answering a few questions about your relationship with Dr Russell?'

'*Mr* Russell—and yes, I would. Get off my ward before I call Security.'

She pushed the trolley into the treatment-room and marched towards the nursing station, the reporter on her heels.

'Is it true that you've been having an affair with him?'

'No, it's not,' she said firmly. 'And I have no further comment. Now get out.'

He went, reluctantly, but he wasn't the last.

Gavin, too, was accosted as he walked along the corridor. He found Helen and Ross in the office and peered under the desk before relaxing with a grin.

'They're everywhere! I daren't even go for a pee in case one of them crawls out of the urinal!'

Helen summoned a faint smile. 'I think you're safe in there, Gavin,' she said.

Ross shook his head. 'Oh, no—I was tracked down in Theatre—the guy all but barged in. Nothing, believe me, is sacred. They want a story, and they don't care what lengths they go to to get it.'

There was a sudden rumpus on the ward, and Ross went out to investigate. Voices were raised, and Helen opened the door and watched as uniformed security staff came from down the corridor and removed another reporter.

'It's ridiculous,' she said furiously. 'How are we supposed to nurse all these sick people in this kind of atmosphere?'

'God knows. Right, I'm going to try and conduct a clinic. Will you be all right?' Ross asked worriedly.

'Of course I'll be all right—it's the reporters you want to worry about.'

Ross's mouth tipped into a grin. 'Attagirl. Right, I'll see you later. Any problems, just ring and I'll come up.'

There were problems, but nothing she could have anticipated. Another stranger appeared on the ward, dressed in a white coat with a stethoscope sticking out of her pocket.

'Sister Cooper?'

She eyed the new doctor cautiously. 'Yes?'

'I'm Mr Henderson's new SHO. Dr Taylor.'

She held out her hand, and Helen shook it, relaxing slightly. Of course she had known of the change, but hadn't realised it was quite so soon. But then, the past few weeks had been enough to confuse her utterly.

'It's a bit crazy in here today, isn't it?' Dr Taylor said.

Helen gave a hollow laugh. 'You haven't chosen the

best day to start on the ward, I have to agree. Still, it will all blow over.'

'Do you think he's innocent?'

'Of course he's innocent,' she said with as much conviction as she could muster.

'But with all that money at stake — well, anyone would be tempted, wouldn't they?'

'I think you'll find he's got more about him than to kill his wife for the life insurance,' she said repressively.

'Oh, no — but then we aren't talking about life insurance, are we? I mean, she's an heiress,' the woman said. 'I thought you would have know that, considering your relationship with Mr Russell.'

Helen shot her a quelling glance. 'I have no relationship with Mr Russell — and if you want to work happily on this ward you'd better learn to keep your mouth shut and your nose to yourself!'

'So it's all conjecture, then? Even though you've been seen together on numerous occasions outside the hospital?'

Helen was suddenly suspicious. 'Look, what the hell is this?' She saw Oliver appear in the background, and as if he could sense trouble he made his way over to them.

'Problems, Sister?'

'Yes, problems with your new SHO, Dr Taylor — if she is your new SHO, which I doubt.'

Oliver eyed her. 'I think not. My new SHO doesn't start until next month, and *he* is Nigerian. Sorry, *Dr* Taylor, you've been rumbled.'

He seized a handful of her white coat and frog-marched her out of the ward, protesting vociferously. Seconds later he was back. 'Are you OK?'

She was shaken. 'I think so. Whatever will they dream up next?'

However, by this time Security had called in more staff and were checking everyone entering and leaving the hospital. They had no more incidents, but Helen was still thoroughly rattled.

So were many of the patients. 'Whoever would have thought it?' Judy Fulcher said. 'He always seemed such a nice man — fancy murdering his wife!'

'He didn't murder her,' Helen said, again with as much conviction as she could muster.

'Couldn't blame him if he did,' Judy went on. 'Fancy her being a vegetable all that time! Mind, I wouldn't agree that he did it for the money — even a rotten judge of character like me could tell that — but plenty of people would — two and a half million, they reckon she was worth.'

Helen was stunned. She stared in amazement, and Judy thrust the paper at her. 'Here, it's all over the front page. Mind, you might not like what you see about yourself — well, I don't know, I suppose some of it might be true, but I think it's going a bit far to say you've been planning it together ——'

Helen snatched the paper and took it into her office, then spread it on the desk with trembling hands. Emblazoned on the front beside a picture of Tom, in huge black letters, were the words COMA HEIRESS DIES — WAS IT MURDER?

She read on, appalled, and found a sordid story of her supposed 'affair' with Tom and a lot of smutty conjecture about them planning Juliette's murder to get their hands on the money.

'I think you'd better have a few days off and hide,' Ross said when he came in.

'No. It would look like an admission of guilt. I'm not skulking in corners. They can say what they like, Ross, I know the truth — and they aren't within a million miles of it.'

Respect showed in his eyes. 'Good girl. Well, if it all gets too much you can come and stay with us. In fact that might be a good idea anyway.'

But again she refused, this time because she didn't want the Press descending on Lizzi and giving her a hard time when she was six months pregnant.

She wondered at the wisdom of her decision, though, later that night when she had to run the gauntlet of the gutter Press to get into her flat.

She refused to turn on the television for the local news and current affairs programme, but watched the BBC nine o'clock news and was appalled to find the story was headlines.

There was an interview with Juliette's family's lawyer, and Helen got the impression that they were out for blood. Certainly the Tom he described wasn't the man she knew and loved.

What must he be feeling now?

She switched off the set, made a drink and went to bed, although she knew there was no danger of her falling asleep. All her thoughts were with Tom.

Had he done it? Certainly not for the money, of that she was convinced, but for Juliette? If so, it must have taken considerable courage.

She wished she could talk to him, find out the truth, but he was still in police custody and it was impossible.

She ran the gauntlet of the Press again in the morning, and arrived on the ward to find the patients buzzing. It was all over the front of the national dailies,

with the tabloids carrying titles like DOCTOR DEATH—
MURDER OR EUTHANASIA?

She was sickened by them, by the muck-raking and
filth, the evil, tortuous minds that must have conjured
the stories out of thin air.

'They make him sound like a serial killer!' she said
furiously to Ross.

'Pay no attention. I won't read it, it's garbage.'

So she took his advice and ignored the papers,
refused to discuss the case with the patients, and
gradually they stopped mentioning it—at least to her.

But she found that every time she approached a
group of people, be it staff or patients, silence fell.

She went home that night and turned on the news,
to find that Tom had been released because the police
lacked evidence.

However, it seemed there was a time lag between
four o'clock when Tom had been seen leaving the clinic
and five-thirty when he'd arrived home, a forty-minute
drive away. He had no alibi for that time, except that
he had apparently stopped at a garage somewhere to
buy petrol. However, he couldn't remember the name
of the garage, or even where it was. Police were
appealing for the man in the garage to contact them,
but so far no one had come forward to corroborate
Tom's story. That was worrying, because apparently
no one had seen Juliette after Tom left until her body
was discovered at five, by which time she had been
dead probably less than half an hour.

That meant, the reporter said, that Tom would have
had time to slip back in, murder his wife and get back
to his cottage by five-thirty.

However, no one had seen him come back in, and so
it was still all a matter of supposition.

They then went on to a discussion of persistent vegetative state and the current medico-legal position, and Helen turned it off.

So he was home—or at least had been allowed to leave the police station. She considered ringing him, and then decided against it. What if his phone was tapped?

She waited until midnight, then checked that there were no reporters lurking around the bushes before getting into her car and driving to Rose Cottage.

There were no reporters there, either, that she could see. She pulled up and got out cautiously, triggering the security lighting.

She was appalled by what she saw. The flowerbeds had been trampled on, one rose pulled off the wall where someone had obviously tried to climb up it to look through the upstairs windows. It had vicious thorns, and she hoped that the person responsible had been well and truly punctured.

There were no lights on inside, and her heart sank. He wasn't here after all. She rang the bell anyway, and called, but with no real hope, and after a few moments she gave up.

She was just getting back into her car when she heard a key scrape in the lock.

'Helen?'

'Tom!'

She spun round and her hand flew up to her mouth. He looked terrible—drawn and haggard, his face etched with tiredness. She stared at him for endless seconds, horrified.

'What's the matter, Helen?' he said, his mouth twisting bitterly. 'Afraid I'll murder you, too?'

She dropped her hand and went towards him. 'Don't be ridiculous. You just look—oh, Tom, I'm so sorry.'

She wanted to hold him, to be held, to feel his arms strong around her, making everything right, but he was remote, his face a mask, colder than she had ever seen it, and she came to a halt a few feet away.

His voice, too, was cold, rigidly controlled. 'I don't think you should be here—the gutter Press would have a field day if they caught you.'

'I just wanted to see you, to make sure you were all right.'

'I'm fine.'

He was clearly not, but she sensed she would get nothing more out of him.

'Call me if you need anything.'

He nodded. 'Give me a few days, Helen. There's a lot to sort out, and I don't think it's a good idea you being around.'

He looked worse close up, his eyes ravaged with emotion. She laid her hand on his arm. 'Tom, I just want you to know I'm here. No matter what, I'll stand by you.'

His eyes searched her face, a quick frown touching his brow. He shook her arm off. 'You think I did it, don't you? You think I killed her.'

She hesitated for a fraction of a second, but it was enough.

Contempt blazed in his eyes—contempt and a terrible despair. 'My God!' he grated. 'How could you? You, of all people! I thought you knew me!'

She faltered under the blistering glare. 'I—I do know you! I certainly know you wouldn't have killed her for the money——'

He snorted. 'Such generosity,' he spat. 'Why then, if not for the money?'

She made herself meet his eyes. 'For love?'

He gave a hollow laugh that chilled her to the bone. 'Oh, my dear, you flatter yourself. I think you ought to go now, before you say anything else.'

'But——'

He turned and let himself back into the house, shutting and locking the door. She heard the bolt slide, and his footsteps as he crossed the kitchen and went upstairs.

'I didn't mean me,' she murmured helplessly. 'Tom, I didn't mean *me*—oh, God! Tom!'

She banged on the door, sobbing and pleading with him, but she was greeted by a stony silence. After a while she was forced to give up, her throat hoarse and her hands bruised from pounding on the wood.

She stumbled back to the car and drove home, her hands trembling on the wheel. Of course she didn't think he'd killed Juliette for her! What did he take her for, for heaven's sake? Didn't he know her better than that?

Obviously not. It seemed they didn't know each other at all, she thought painfully, but two things she was convinced of now. The first was that he was innocent—not only of murdering Juliette for her money, but of murdering her at all. The second was that if they had ever stood a chance she had just blown it into smithereens.

The Press must have got hold of him the following day, because the evening papers were full of pictures of him trying to leave the cottage, and he was on the local evening news programme.

His only replies had apparently been 'no comment' — until they asked about Helen. Then he had told them that she was nothing more to him than a colleague.

It was a stock response, and only what she had been saying herself all week, but something in his eyes as he looked at the camera told her that he really meant it, and the last glimmer of hope flickered and died.

Tom didn't return to work for the whole of that week. The funeral would be delayed until the coroner released Juliette's body, and until then he was on what the management committee referred to as 'compassionate leave'.

Helen was sure it was a form of suspension, that as long as he was under suspicion he wouldn't be returning, and there seemed no way he could prove his innocence.

And then, towards the end of the week, the man working in the garage came forward and said he remembered seeing Tom. 'It was four-thirty, near enough, because that's when we close and I was just about to shut off the power to the pumps when he turned in. I remember him, because he looked sort of sad — as if he had the cares of the world on his shoulders.'

He hadn't come forward before, apparently, because he was moonlighting on social security. If he hadn't had a conscience Tom might have ended up in prison for a crime he hadn't committed, the reporter said, because the garage was some twenty-five minutes from the clinic by the shortest route, and so after filling up the car, which must have taken several minutes, Tom couldn't have got back there before five o'clock, the time Juliette was found to have died.

Her death was due to asphyxia, and had probably

been caused by her head rolling forward on the pillow. She had sometimes made involuntary movements, the reporter revealed, and it was possible that she had suffocated herself inadvertently.

So that was the end of that. Tom was in the clear.

It was a relief to have it confirmed, but she had known from the look in his eyes that he was innocent.

If only she hadn't said anything!

The funeral was held on Tuesday, and the Press were there at their scurrilous best.

One local paper caught her eye — a photograph of Tom, staring down into Juliette's grave, his face etched with pain, and another photograph, this time of flowers, a brilliant spray of jewel colours, and a card which read, 'Juliette, May you find peace at last, My love, Tom.'

Helen wept for him.

He was back on Wednesday, grim-faced and silent, and everyone kept out of his way.

Nobody knew how to talk to him, whether to offer their condolences on the death of his wife, relief that he had been cleared, horror that the Press had been so unfair, or just simply say nothing.

By and large they said nothing. Ross spoke to him, of course, a few quiet words alone, but he looked straight through Helen as if she didn't exist, and she could have wept.

He threw himself back into his work, and after a few days the dust seemed to settle and everything got back to normal.

Everything, that was, except for his relationship with Helen. That remained as economical and professional as possible, and it hurt more than she would have believed.

Judy Fulcher left — not to her old home, but with her new partner. She would divorce her husband, she said, and they were to get married.

Helen was glad someone was having a happy ending. She, for one, was desperately unhappy, and if his face was anything to go by so was Tom.

He was thinner, his cheeks sunken, and if his eyes had looked haunted before they were tortured now.

Helen had seen grief in the past, but never had it struck her so forcibly as it did then. If only there was something she could do, some way to help him.

She realised that he would want nothing to do with her in any romantic sense — any fool could see that, looking at him — but if she could only persuade him to listen to her, to let her explain what she had meant, then perhaps they could go back to what they had had before.

Perhaps, just perhaps, she could help him to weather the grief of his loss.

She had no hope that she could ever win his heart. That lay with his beautiful butterfly, but maybe she could help to ease the pain.

And then, every time she saw him and he looked right through her, her courage failed.

Towards the end of August, nearly four weeks after Juliette's death, a woman was admitted with recurrent haematemesis. She had vomited blood again that morning, and her GP had admitted her direct. Her abdomen was swollen and distended with fluid, and her liver was slightly enlarged and tender. She was also, according to her husband, a heavy drinker and had been for years.

'She's almost certainly got oesophageal varices —

looking at her I'd say she's got cirrhosis of the liver, and she's got other symptoms of portal hypertension like the swollen abdomen. I gather from her husband she's a bit of a soak, so I wouldn't be surprised, but I think we ought to do something before those veins in her oesphagus burst terminally,' Tom told Ross.

They were in Helen's office, and she was sitting at the desk trying to catch up on the paperwork. She could see Tom out of the corner of her eye, and she found it highly distracting.

Ross was agreeing with Tom and suggesting surgery for the woman that morning. 'Right, I must get on. Can I leave her to you?'

Tom nodded, and Helen waited until Ross left before lifting her head.

'Tom?' she said softly.

He turned towards her, his eyes cold. 'What?'

Her courage failed. 'Nothing. Forget it.' She drew a deep, steadying breath. 'Do you want me to prepare Mrs Sykes for Theatre straight away, or do you want to talk to her first?'

'I'll talk to her, but I don't want to hang about. I'd like to have another look now she's settled in the ward, but I think we've got to act fast. You'd better come.'

Helen stood up and went with him, conscious of his grudging request, as if he would rather have had a ward orderly assist him than her.

Mrs Sykes was propped up in bed, her face pale under the jaundice. There was a faint sheen of sweat on her brow, and Tom exchanged glances with Helen.

'I think you'd better prep her now; she looks even worse,' he murmured.

Her husband sat beside her holding her hand, and as they approached she laid her hand over her stomach and groaned. 'Oh, love, I'm going to be sick again,' she said tremulously, and then she sat upright and blood gushed out of her mouth, flooding over the bed and spreading in a pool on the floor.

Within seconds she was dead.

There was a shocked silence on the ward, and then the staff all leapt into action. Tom took her weight off her husband and eased her back on to the pillows, Helen whisked the curtains round the bed, and Ruth appeared with a clean blanket and dropped it over the pool of blood.

Mr Sykes was shaking uncontrollably, his hands and chest covered in blood, and Ruth found another blanket and laid it over his shoulders, then covered Mrs Sykes below the chin, discreetly wiping her mouth with a corner of the sheet.

Helen could hear the rest of her staff making soothing noises and calming the shocked patients, and she put her arm around Mr Sykes and led him away to her office.

He was absolutely devastated, and it took all Helen's considerable skill and compassion to deal with him.

After a short while Tom appeared, without his white coat.

'How is he?' he asked softly.

'Very shocked.'

'I'm not surprised.' He crouched down by the trembling man and took his hand. 'Mr Sykes?'

The man met his eyes, dazed.

'She's dead?'

Tom nodded. 'Yes, I'm afraid so. She had a burst blood vessel. If it's any consolation, she would hardly have suffered anything.'

Mr Sykes shuddered. 'Where is she?'

'They've taken her to the Chapel of Rest — if you'd like to see her, I'm sure someone can take you down.'

He nodded slowly, then covered his face and wept, harsh, racking sobs that ripped out of his chest. 'I always knew it'd be the death of her,' he said finally. 'She would have it. "Just a bit of stout, love," she'd say, and over the years it grew more and more —'

He covered his face again, and Tom straightened and looked at Helen. 'Could you sort out someone to take him down?'

'I'll take him. Come on, Mr Sykes. Let's wash your hands and take off your jacket — Tom, there's a brown paper bag in that cupboard; could you get it for me?'

She folded the jacket and put it in the bag, then wiped his hands with damp paper towels before taking him down to the Chapel of Rest.

He was joined there a short while later by his daughter, and Helen left them together and went back up to the ward.

Tom was still there, filling in Mrs Sykes's records.

'Poor man. What a terrible shock.'

'At least it was quick,' he said economically, and shut the file. 'Right, I suppose I'd better go home.'

He walked away, his face bleak. Clearly home held no great attractions for him any more. Helen wondered what he was doing with himself in the evenings, how he passed the endless, lonely hours.

And suddenly she knew she couldn't put it off any more. She had to talk to him, and she had to do it today.

Her heart pounding in her chest, she turned into Tom's drive and switched off the engine.

The garden still showed faint traces of the damage

the reporters had done. The rose had been put back up, but much of it had been cut away and many of the beds had empty patches or broken shrubs.

Like life, she thought. Once things are done, you can try and clear up the mess but there are still scars. She wondered how effective her own clearing-up operation with Tom would be. She had no great hopes.

He opened the door just as she reached for the bell, and stood in the doorway regarding her impassively.

'Yes?'

She closed her eyes. 'Tom, please — I have to talk to you. I can't bear it any more — '

'What are you here for, Helen? The money?'

Her eyes flew open. 'You're contemptible!' she whispered. 'I care nothing for your money — '

'That's a good job, because there isn't any,' he said harshly. 'It's all in a trust fund, and it's being used to set up a children's hospital in India.'

'Juliette's dream,' she said numbly.

'Exactly. So, if it's not the money, what is it?'

She sighed shakily. 'I wanted to explain — you misunderstood — '

'I don't think so. You believe I murdered Juliette — '

'No! No, I never believed you murdered her. I was very much afraid that you might have done, but not for me. I'm not that egotistical and vain, as you should well know.'

'I thought I did. So why should I murder her? You said I'd killed her for love — funny sort of love.'

She took a deep breath. 'Not really. You said months ago, when you asked Ross to let Ron Church die, that there was more to life than a beating heart. Only the week before Juliette died you said that you hated to see her so lifeless, that you knew if she had any awareness she would have hated to be trapped like that. You said you didn't want her to die, but you wished it could be over. And then, suddenly, it was.'

'And you thought I might have done it? To get it over?'

'For her,' she said earnestly. 'The one last thing you could do for her — to set her free.'

'And you would have condoned that?' His voice was harsh.

'No! No, not condoned — but I would have understood, knowing how it hurt you to see her suffer, knowing how you still loved her.'

His voice softened. 'What makes you think I loved her?'

'You said — again, on that day — that you didn't feel you could make a sound decision about her future if you were asked to, because your judgement was clouded by love.'

He was very still, not even breathing for a moment, and then, very slowly, his hand came up and cupped her cheek. 'Love for you, Helen. My love for Juliette died a long time ago. You're all that matters to me now.'

'You love me?' Helen was incredulous. She looked up and met his eyes. 'But you've been so cruel——' Her eyes blurred, and she turned away, unable to believe him. 'How can you say you love me when you've been so cold and unkind?'

His voice was hesitant, filled with regret. 'I thought I'd made a mistake — thought you weren't the person I imagined you were. Perhaps I'd made you into something you weren't, just to fill the lonely ache in my heart. I was still very shocked, and when I realised you thought that of me I was angry. Very angry. Angry that you could think it of me, and angry that you could possibly stand by me if I had killed her. It only hurt so badly because I loved you and needed you so much. Helen, I'm sorry. Forgive me.'

She turned back to him. His face was no longer a mask, but a window on his soul, and all the loneliness and suffering were clear to see. So, also, was his love.

'Oh, Tom — I thought it was too late —'

Suddenly she was in his arms, held firmly against his chest, and all the dammed-up pain and sorrow of the past few months came pouring out.

Finally the tears slowed, and Tom tilted her head back and kissed away the tears.

'Oh, Helen. I was so sure I'd lost you, that you were just a dream conjured out of my loneliness. I don't deserve you.'

'Tough,' she said tremulously, 'because you're stuck with me.'

'You'd better come in, then,' he said, and his lips quirked into that lovely, fleeting smile.

Her heart kicked again.

'I love you, Tom Russell,' she murmured as he shut the door and drew her into his arms again.

'Oh, Helen, I love you, too — so very, very much. Will you marry me, when all the dust has settled and things are back to normal?'

'Oh, Tom, I'd be proud to.'

'Silly girl,' he said gruffly, and brushed her lips with his.

She gave a shaky little laugh. 'I know can't compare with Juliette — I'm not as pretty, and I'm not very efficient, and you'll never lose me in Marrakech, because I'm too much of a coward, but I will try hard to be a good wife to you, Tom.'

His eyes filled with tears. 'Oh, Helen, you still don't understand, do you?' he said tenderly. 'Juliette was hell to live with. Yes, I loved her, but it waş a very masochistic process. But you — you're like the rain after drought, like a cool breeze on a hot day — I don't think you have any idea how much I love you.'

'You gave up so easily, though. As if you were looking for a way out — ' Her voice broke, and the tears spilt again.

'I don't want a way out,' he said raggedly. 'Helen, come to bed — please? Let me show you how much I love you?'

She hesitated, afraid to disappoint him.

'What's wrong?' he asked softly.

'I'm not — I haven't done this much,' she confessed. 'Juliette — '

'Helen, stop it! Juliette's dead. To all intents and purposes, she's been dead for years. I know I can't forget her, and I wouldn't want to, but she's gone, and I've learned to deal with that. I did my grieving for her three years ago, Helen. I'm ready to go on now — with you.'

She looked up, her face radiant through the tears, and held out her hand. He took it, and lifted it to his lips, his eyes holding hers. 'I love you, Helen.'

'I love you, too, Tom — more than I can ever say.'

'Come on.' His voice was gruff, and he meshed his fingers with hers and led her up the narrow little stairs to his bedroom.

There he undressed her, slowly and tenderly, tutting over how thin she was, and then he laid her on the bed and stripped off his clothes and lay down beside her.

She could hardly breathe, and, as his hand came up and brushed her tears away, their lips met, and clung.

'I've wanted you for so long I'm almost afraid to touch you,' he murmured.

'Please touch me,' she begged. 'I need you, Tom. Please?'

There were no rockets, no shooting stars or freefall through the planets.

Just Tom, holding her close, loving her from the bottom of his heart.

It was all she could ever ask, and as the passion built and shattered Helen knew he was all she would ever need, for the rest of their lives together.

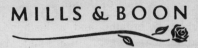

MILLS & BOON

Proudly present...

CHARLOTTE LAMB'S ♥ 100th ♥ ROMANCE

This is a remarkable achievement for a writer who had her first Mills & Boon novel published in 1973. Some six million words later and with sales around the world, her novels continue to be popular with romance fans everywhere.

Her centenary romance *'VAMPIRE LOVER'* is a suspense-filled story of dark desires and tangled emotions—Charlotte Lamb at her very best.

Published: June 1994   **Price: £1.90**

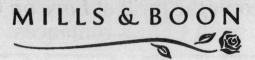

MILLS & BOON

Discover the thrill of *Love on Call* with 4 FREE romances

BOOKS FOR YOU

In the exciting world of modern medicine, the emotions of true love acquire an added poignancy. Now you can experience these gripping stories of passion and pain, heartbreak and happiness - with Mills & Boon absolutely FREE! AND look forward to a regular supply of *Love on Call* delivered direct to your door.

🌹 🌹 🌹

Turn the page for details of how to claim 4 FREE books AND 2 FREE gifts!

An irresistible offer from Mills & Boon

Here's a very special offer from Mills & Boon for you to become a regular reader of *Love on Call*. And we'd like to welcome you with 4 books, a cuddly teddy bear and a special mystery gift - absolutely FREE and without obligation!

Then, every month look forward to receiving 4 brand new *Love on Call* romances delivered direct to your door for only £1.80 each. Postage and packing is FREE!

Plus a FREE Newsletter featuring authors, competitions, special offers and lots more...

This invitation comes with no strings attached. You may cancel or suspend your subscription at any time and still keep your FREE books and gifts.

It's so easy. Send no money now but simply complete the coupon below and return it today to:

Mills & Boon Reader Service, FREEPOST, PO Box 236, Croydon, Surrey CR9 9EL.

--- **NO STAMP NEEDED** --- ✂

YES! Please rush me 4 FREE *Love on Call* romances and 2 FREE gifts! Please also reserve me a Reader Service subscription. If I decide to subscribe, I can look forward to receiving 4 brand new *Love on Call* romances for only £7.20 every month - postage and packing FREE. If I choose not to subscribe, I shall write to you within 10 days and still keep the FREE books and gifts. I may cancel or suspend my subscription at any time simply be writing to you. I am over 18 years of age.   Please write in BLOCK CAPITALS

Ms/Mrs/Miss/Mr _____ EP62D

Address _____

_____

_____ Postcode _____

Signature _____

Offer closes 30th September 1994. The right is reserved to refuse an application and change the terms of this offer. One application per household. Offer not valid to current Love on Call subscribers. Offer valid only in UK and Eire. Overseas readers please write for details. Southern Africa write to IBS, Private Bag, X3010, Randburg, 2125, South Africa. You may be mailed with offers from other reputable companies as a result of this application. Please tick box if you would prefer not to receive such offers. ☐

mps
MAILING PREFERENCE SERVICE